TUMBLING INTO TOMORROW

A SMALL TOWN CHRISTIAN ROMANCE

LOVE ON SANCTUARY SHORES
BOOK ONE

JULIETTE DUNCAN

NOTE FROM THE AUTHOR:

HELLO! Thank you for choosing to read this book - I hope you enjoy it! *Tumbling into Tomorrow* is Book One in the multi-author series, *Love on Sanctuary Shores*, which includes the following titles:

Tumbling into Tomorrow by Juliette Duncan
Fighting for Her Heart by Tara Grace Ericson
Surrendering to Love by Kristen M Fraser
Running into Forever by Jennifer Rodewald
Trusting His Promise by Valerie M Bodden
Wishing for Mistletoe by Robin Lee Hatcher

You'll find more details at the end of the story.

As a thank you for reading this book, I'd like to offer you a FREE GIFT. That's right - my FREE novella, "Hank and Sarah - A Love Story" is available exclusively to my newsletter subscribers. Go to: http://www.julietteduncan. com/subscribe claim your copy now and to be notified of my future book releases. I hope you enjoy both books!

Blessings,
Juliette

CHAPTER 1

*N*ate Hawthorn opened his front door and stepped onto his porch, rubbing his gloved hands together while breathing in the frigid air as he waited for his five-year-old daughter, Emma, to join him. Snow blanketed the ground, weighing down every bough and dressing the naked tree limbs under tiny crystals. Through the trees and between the houses, the ice-covered Lake Huron stretched into the distance, glistening under the morning sun.

A lifelong resident, Nate loved Sanctuary Island, especially in midwinter when, for a few months each year, the residents got to enjoy their little piece of paradise without sharing it with the hordes of tourists who flocked there each summer. Not that he minded them—the wealthy tourists kept his business afloat—but he loved this slower pace.

The door opened, and Emma slipped her small hand into his. "Can we go now, Daddy?"

"Sure, sweetheart." He squeezed her hand and closed the door.

"Look at all this snow! How are we going to get down?" Awe widened her brown eyes.

Nate grimaced. He should have been out here shoveling instead of playing games with his daughter, but what was more important? Besides, they weren't snowed in yet. "Good question. What do you think?"

"Stomp across it?"

"Great plan. Let's go." Sweeping her into his arms, he launched into the soft snow and sank deep to his knees.

Emma's giggles warmed his heart. Now that Bethany was gone, Emma was the light of his life. With curly brown hair framing her pixie face, light brown eyes, and a smile that chased his melancholy away, his daughter was so like his late wife it hurt. Five years after her passing, he still missed her terribly, and despite the joy Emma brought him each day and the satisfaction he had in the life he gave her, something was missing—a nagging feeling deep inside that refused to go away. He pushed it to the back of his mind, as he usually did, and focused instead on the beauty around him. And on his daughter.

"That was fun! Can we do it again?" Emma's eyes sparkled above her deep dimples.

"Maybe, but not now. We've got to get you to Grandma's so Daddy can go to work."

"Okay." She pouted but hugged tight around his neck.

At the end of their walkway, he set her on the ground and took her hand, swinging their arms between them as she began skipping along the cleared sidewalk. "Daddy, what's that sound?"

"Horned larks. Can you see them up there on the branch?" He pointed upward to where two small birds sat on a snow-covered limb.

She lifted her gaze. "They must be cold."

"They have feathers to keep them warm. God looks after them really well."

"Just like you look after me."

He gulped as his chest constricted under the weight of that responsibility. Thank God for his mother. Without her support, he doubted he could have cared for the tiny baby he was left with when Bethany died of cancer mere days after Emma was born. "I do my best, sweetie."

They headed alongside a road devoid of cars because many years ago the residents voted to remove them from the town center—a great decision that gave the place a special feel.

Max Holden, Nate's fifty-five-year-old neighbor, was bent over his shovel clearing snow from his walkway. As they approached, he straightened and offered a friendly smile. "Hey there, neighbor! How goes the day?"

"Pretty good so far. Heavy snowfall last night, though."

Max leaned on his shovel and palmed the back of his neck. "Yes, and they say there's more on the way. Best get it shoveled before I can't get out. Can't afford to be housebound."

"Absolutely." Nate glanced back at his own walkway and grimaced. He must clear it, and soon, or he and Emma could be stuck inside all winter.

Max cleared his throat. "How's your mom? I haven't seen her in a while."

Nate stifled a chuckle. Although Max was a confirmed bachelor, Nate suspected his neighbor was sweet on Mom, who seemed oblivious to his affection. "Mom's fine, but she's focused on her quilting project and hasn't stepped out much."

"Ah, yes." Max gave a sage nod and twisted the edge of his mustache. "The quilting project. I'm looking forward to seeing the finished product revealed at the Annual Extravaganza. Your mother always knows how to bring this town together."

Indeed. Her community spirit was shared by all, and when she came up with an idea, others happily joined in the venture. It was how things worked on Sanctuary Island. Everyone was there for everyone else.

"That she does. And speaking of which, I need to drop Emma off. I've got a long day, and I'm running late."

"Don't let me keep you, then. Give Grace my regards and tell her I'll be expecting some of her famous sugar cookies next time I see her." Max winked, and one corner of his mouth pulled into a would-be boyish grin—if the mustache hadn't wrecked the effect.

Yep, he was sweet on Mom. "Sure thing. Take it easy, Max." Nate raised a friendly hand and waved, then continued walking, Emma's hand once again securely tucked into his.

"Bye, Uncle Max!" she called out while waving her other hand and skipping backward.

"Bye, Emma. Have a great day."

She faced forward and continued skipping as they headed north along Superior Street. Just past the Lutheran Church, Mrs. Thomassen strode toward them, her brightly colored scarf flapping in the wind like a windsock, while Mitchell, her border collie, charged ahead. Who was walking whom, Nate wasn't sure, but Mrs. Thomassen looked like the one getting the larger workout. He greeted her with a smile. She returned the gesture but kept half walking, half running to keep up with her dog.

"I like Mitchell. Can we get a dog, Daddy?" Emma lifted her pixie face and gave him puppy-dog eyes.

"One day, sweetheart."

"When I'm six?"

They crossed Fourth Street, and he was about to give his standard answer of "maybe" when his mother waved to them from her front porch. "Nate! Emma!"

Dropping his hand, Emma sprinted along the walkway, climbed the steps, and threw herself into his mother's open arms.

"There's my princess." Mom kissed the top of Emma's head, a smile broadening her round face.

The pair's special relationship, forged through shared loss following his dad's untimely death three months before Bethany's, always warmed Nate's heart. God seemingly provided Emma to fill the hole their passing had left. But why had God allowed them both to die in the first place? Yeah. Nate still struggled with that, although he rarely spoke about it, even at the Thursday night support group he occasionally attended.

As he strolled along the snow-free walkway toward the house, his brow creased. "Who cleared your walkway?"

Mom shrugged. "Not sure. I found it that way when I came out. Good Samaritan, I suppose. Though I would have liked it if they'd said something. I could've made them some hot chocolate as a thank you."

Nate chuckled. Perhaps Max Holden had been shoveling snow since the crack of dawn. It wouldn't surprise him.

"Speaking of hot chocolate, would you like one before you head off?"

"Sounds good, but I'd best get going. Busy day ahead. I'll pick Emma up around five."

Mom placed her hands on Emma's shoulders. "See you later, then. And take care. The weather report said more snow could be on the way."

He kissed her cheek before crouching and hugging his daughter. Sometimes, Mom treated him as if he were still a child who needed her words of warning, but he loved that she loved him enough to do it. "I'll be careful, but you should stay safe and warm inside."

"That's my plan!"

After she ushered Emma inside, he turned on his heel and strolled down the sidewalk toward the communal parking lot to pick up his Ski-Doo. Although sometimes inconvenient, he liked that motorized vehicles weren't allowed in the town proper. Plus, it helped that the parking lot was on his side of town.

At the lot, he headed straight for the back row where his blue and black snowmobile was lined up amongst other similar ones. He removed the cover and straddled it. Slipping on his helmet, he primed the engine and hit the start switch.

After the engine roared to life, he headed cross-country to Elijah's Garage and Workshop, a hundred yards along the airport road on the outskirts of town. He pulled up outside the dedicated snowmobile bay, removed his helmet, and strode inside. The clatter of tools and the hum of machinery echoed through the workshop filled with various projects in different stages of repair, from dismantled snowmobiles to half-assembled engines.

Rodney, the apprentice mechanic, was bent over one of those engines.

"Hey, Rodney, do you know where Elijah is?"

The young man straightened and pointed over his shoulder. "In the office, I think."

Nate nodded his thanks and strolled across the concrete floor toward the enclosed space at the rear. Seated behind a desk littered with papers and tools, Elijah was cradling his phone in his neck while he wiped his hands with a rag. "Yes, I can pick up some milk on the way home. And I haven't forgotten it's movie night. I'll grab some snacks. Okay. I love you, too. Bye."

After fifteen years of marriage, Elijah and Sarah were still as affectionate as when they met in college. Nate braced a shoulder against the doorjamb. Would he and Bethany still be that close had she lived? Sadly, no amount of pondering would bring her back.

Elijah ended the call and waved him in. "Didn't expect to see you this morning, but come in. Do you want a drink?"

"No, but thanks." Nate looped his thumbs in his belt. "I was just wondering if you had time to give Clarabel a quick once-over. A large group's coming in tomorrow, and I don't want any surprises."

Elijah scratched his head and looked at his screen. "Didn't I check her when I did the other machines last week?"

"No. I was out inspecting the trail that day and didn't get back in time."

"That's right. I remember." Elijah jumped to his feet and rounded the desk. "No worries. I'll look at her now."

"Sure you got the time?"

Elijah clapped his shoulder. "Always got time for you, Nate."

Something warmed inside Nate as they headed into the workshop side by side. Good friends like Elijah were hard to come by, and he'd never take their friendship for granted.

Passing a new silver-gray Chevy Colorado, Nate paused and ran his hand along its side. "She's a beauty."

Elijah folded his arms. "Belonged to Wolfgang Hammersmith. His son asked me to check it over before he takes it to the mainland to sell in the spring."

"Such a pity Wolfgang didn't make it through his cancer treatment."

"Yeah. A real pity. He was so confident he'd beat it."

Nate's shoulders drooped. Just like Bethany. Right to her final breath, she believed God would heal her. That's what they'd been praying for, but it wasn't to be. Mom told him God *did* heal her, just not in the way they'd all expected. Nate still had words with God about that.

He followed Elijah outside.

His friend turned to him. "How's Emma? Still planning on being Sanctuary Island's next big artist?"

Nate waved a hand. "That was last month. This month she's into science. Says she wants to study the stars."

Elijah pushed Nate's Ski-Doo inside and began his inspection. "Never too young to dream big."

"Sometimes I wonder what she'll be when she grows up. Then I tell myself not to rush it, but to simply enjoy this time with her."

"She'll grow up too quickly. They all do. Tina's only twelve, but she acts like she's eighteen." Elijah switched sides and crouched down again.

Nate leaned against the Colorado in the next bay, his arms folded as he released a heavy breath. "I sure hope I'm doing it right. There's so much I don't know. Things

9

Bethany would've taught her. I'm trying my best, but I never know if it's enough."

Elijah glanced at him and then back at the Ski-Doo. "You're fortunate your mom's around to help."

"You can say that again." His mother had given up her position as a teacher at the local school to care for Emma after Bethany died. He wouldn't have survived without her help.

Moments passed. "You know, you don't have to stay single for the rest of your life."

Nate shoved his hands in his pockets and released a heavy breath. "Between Emma and the center, there's not much room for anything else. Besides, who would I date?"

Straightening, Elijah closed the hood and eyed him. "That's just an excuse—you could make room if you wanted to, and I know, for a fact, you're a contender for being Sanctuary Island's hottest bachelor, even though technically you're a widower."

And therein lay the issue. Despite the loneliness, how could Nate consider dating anyone else? Bethany had been the love of his life. His soulmate. How could he even consider it?

He shifted his gaze from Elijah and palmed his neck. "It's hard, you know. After everything with Bethany—"

"She would've wanted you to be happy."

The words hung in the air. Of course, Elijah was right. Bethany would've wanted him to live his best life, but somehow it seemed wrong to think about loving another woman. God would have to bring someone extra special into his life for him to take even the first step, let alone consider marriage.

Nope, he was happy enough as he was. His life on the island, surrounded by family and friends, was full.

Yeah, who was he kidding? He was lonely. He just wouldn't admit it to anyone.

Elijah wiped his hands on a rag and changed the subject. "Clarabel should be fine until the spring. Keep an eye on the fuel mix in the cold, but you know that."

"Yeah, I do. I appreciate you looking at her."

"What are best buddies for?" Elijah clapped him on the shoulder.

Nate smiled before pushing Clarabel toward the bay doors. As he climbed on, he looked back. "Tell Sarah and the kids I said hello."

"I will. Don't be a stranger."

"I'll pop by sometime soon with Emma."

"Be sure you do. Ride carefully." Elijah raised his hand and headed inside.

Nate slipped on his helmet, revved the engine, zoomed away from the garage, and headed cross-country toward the airport. He should be going the other way, toward the Sanctuary Outdoor Activity Center he owned and managed, but he wanted to give Clarabel a run to make sure she was primed and ready in case of an emergency. Although the island was small, about four miles across the middle and two miles north to south, visitors still occasionally managed to get lost in the state park. Not that many came in winter, and those who did were usually experienced cross-country skiers, but it always paid to be ready, just in case.

Clarabel responded smoothly as he navigated through the powdery snow, staying close to Horizon Road. The island was a winter wonderland with snow-covered pines and a crisp, clear sky. As he sped along, the cold wind nipped at his face through his helmet, and the rhythmic roar of the engine filled the tranquil landscape. Despite the island's small size, its rugged beauty never failed to captivate him.

At the airport—a single runway and a small single-story building that was very quiet at this time of year, with just one flight per day to bring supplies and mail to and from the mainland when the weather allowed, and the odd charter flight—he turned around and headed back to town.

Skirting the outer perimeter, he parked on East Fifth Street opposite the Eastside Café, the only place to get a coffee and bagel at this time of year.

He pushed open one of the double glass doors and strolled inside. Mrs. Larsen, one of the town's older residents, was sitting alone in a booth near the window. He raised his hand at Winona behind the counter and mouthed "the usual, thanks," before strolling over to the elderly lady's table.

"Mrs. Larsen, what are you doing sitting here alone? Where's Mrs. Sumpter?"

She peered at him over the rim of her large-framed glasses, her silver hair pulled into a tight bun atop her head. "Poor dear's caught a cold and decided to stay indoors, but I thought I'd come anyway." She waved to the seat opposite. "Why don't you join me instead?"

Nate grimaced. "I'd love to, but I've got a busy day."

"Come on. Just for a few minutes. I'd love the company."

Since no one argued with Mrs. Larsen, he slid onto the seat as Winona arrived with his order, a turkey-cheese bagel packed neatly in a brown paper sack and a coffee to go, its steam rising in swirls from the spout on the lid. He handed Winona twenty bucks and thanked her.

When she left, Mrs. Larsen leaned forward, her eyes bright behind her glasses. "Did you hear the news?"

"What news?" He leaned back and sipped his coffee.

"We've got a newcomer. Miriam Solheim's great-niece is coming to mind her house while she's away on the mainland. Mrs. Stewart told me this morning when she came in for a coffee and donut."

Nate's brow knit. Miriam Solheim's great-niece. "Harper Mackenzie?"

Mrs. Larsen shrugged. "I'm not sure of her name. All I know is she's arriving today and Max Holden's collecting her from the mainland."

Funny. Max hadn't mentioned anything this morning. He'd quiz his neighbor when he got home. But then Nate stopped. Why was he even interested? Last time he saw Harper Mackenzie, she was a kid at summer camp. A good-looking kid, but a kid.

But that was fifteen years ago. She'd be a grown woman now.

He shook his head. What was he doing?

He pushed to his feet. "Sorry to leave so soon, but work calls. I'll swing by your place later this week and check on you."

"That would be wonderful." The elderly woman clasped his hand with her wrinkled one. "Be sure to bring Emma. I love it when you bring her."

"No problem at all. She loves visiting you."

With his promise given, he exited the café, fired up Clarabel, and headed toward the lake before turning right onto Harbor Way, keeping to the side where the snow was thick. Although the island's outer roads were cleared each morning, most folk preferred to zip around on snowmobiles or skis. He sure did.

Situated just outside the town center on the lake's edge, the Sanctuary Outdoor Activities Center was in a perfect position for both summer and winter sports. He could easily have walked from his house, but where was the fun in that? He parked Clarabel and strolled inside right at nine o'clock.

CHAPTER 2

*H*arper Mackenzie glanced at her watch for the umpteenth time and harrumphed as she peered out the window of the Lakeside Café at Havensport on the shore of Lake Huron. The message had said ten a.m. The man was late. But he lived on an island, and he *was* driving across the ice to collect her, so she stuffed her impatience back inside. This trip was all about letting go, and this was the first test.

No more schedules to keep, no more grueling practice sessions. No more watching everything she ate. No more appeasing Troy.

This was the start of rediscovering Harper Mackenzie. And what better place to do that than on Sanctuary Island, the haven holding wonderful memories of a carefree childhood? Well, it would have been carefree if her parents hadn't sent her to summer camp simply so they didn't need to bother with her.

But during those summers on the island, she'd discovered her love for dance. Who would have thought a performance at a summer-camp concert could have led to her becoming the principal dancer for the Royal Canadian Ballet Company?

But now, thanks to Troy, her career might be over.

She pressed her fist against her mouth and gritted her teeth against the tears stinging her eyes. She wouldn't give in to them. Not this time. The last time she'd given free rein to her heartache, her tears had almost strangled her. She wouldn't go back there. Except, how did she close the floodgates when an entire sea of raw regret and heartache pounded against them?

She should have seen through his charm and realized he didn't love her—she was simply one of the many dancers he'd wined, dined, and flattered over the years.

The apron-clad server appeared at her table, holding a coffeepot. "Would you like a refill, dear?"

Harper shook her head and pushed back her tears. "No, but thanks. My ride should be here any minute."

"Okay. Let me know if you change your mind."

Harper managed a smile and a polite thank you.

Ten minutes later, a snowmobile towing an empty trailer pulled up outside the café. A short, gray-haired man with a mustache jumped off and headed inside. That must be him. Max Holden.

Harper pushed to her feet and collected her bags from behind the counter, thanking the server for minding them.

The woman smiled and wished her good luck as she nodded toward the lake.

Yikes. If she needed good luck, perhaps she should have spent the money and chartered a plane instead of crossing the ice on a snowmobile. But it was too late now because the man was approaching, plus she'd also prepaid.

"Harper Mackenzie?"

With a nod, she shook his outstretched hand. "In the flesh!"

She stifled a groan at the trill in her voice. It had to be the thought of crossing the ice. Aunt Miriam had told her it was safe and Max Holden was the best driver to take her across, but still. When she'd come to summer camp, she'd caught the ferry, which had been fun and safe, but midwinter, everything was different. Had she been foolish in offering to mind Aunt Miram's house and cat? But she couldn't have stayed in Toronto. She needed to get away. Figure things out.

"Max Holden. Nice to meet you. Are these all your bags?" The man reached for the two largest.

"I believe so." She counted them silently. Two large and three small. Yes, they were all there.

"Let's go, then." He wheeled the bags outside and lifted them all onto the trailer before covering them with a tarpaulin. "Ever been on a snowmobile before?"

"Not recently, but yes. I'm looking forward to it." Liar. She was scared stiff.

"Good. Put this helmet on and make sure your jacket's

zipped. It can get chilly out there on the lake, especially if the wind's blowing."

"And is it?"

He grabbed his helmet, snugging it in place, but not flipping the visor down yet. "Not at the moment."

"Good."

"Let me know if you need to stop. Otherwise, it'll take about twenty minutes to cross. Any questions?"

She inhaled deeply and swung her gaze to the ice-covered lake. "Just one. How safe is it?"

"Well, we haven't lost anyone lately. It's safe enough. Don't you worry."

"You… you mean, someone's actually fallen through?"

The man's expression fell. "I'm sorry. I shouldn't have been flippant. No one's fallen through in my knowledge. Although way back, a group of youths thought they were invincible. Decided to be the first to cross before the ice was solid and the bridge was officially opened. They almost didn't make it back."

"Oh. But it's solid now?"

"There's at least twelve inches of ice all the way across, so yes. I wouldn't risk my own life if it wasn't."

Harper drew another long breath. "Okay. Let's do this."

"Good girl." His warm smile gave her confidence.

At his instruction, she straddled the snowmobile and sat behind him, although her heart was beating erratically like it always did before she stepped onto the stage.

He flipped his visor down. "Ready?"

She nodded and tightened her grip on the side handles as the snowmobile roared to life, its powerful engine cutting through the quiet of the snowy landscape. The vast expanse of Lake Huron stretched before her, a sheet of ice shimmering under the pale winter sun. The breath-taking scenery chased away her fears.

As they sped across the frozen lake, the snowmobile's rhythmic thrum became a comforting background hum. With the air crisp and clear, each breath felt like a refreshing gulp of pure life. Snowflakes, light as whispers, danced around them, adding a touch of magic to the stark, wintry landscape. The ice bridge confirmed nature's power and resilience, a crystalline pathway leading to a place of refuge and renewal.

Or at least, so she hoped.

The island loomed in the distance, a dark silhouette against the white expanse. Happy summers spent on its shores warmed her memories, a mix of bittersweet nostalgia and promising new beginnings. Each passing moment brought her closer to rediscovering herself, to healing the wounds left by a love gone sour.

Her thoughts drifted to Aunt Miriam's cozy home, the welcoming warmth that awaited her, and the serenity she hoped to find. The snowmobile's rhythmic motion and the enchanting winter landscape created a sense of peace, a stark contrast to the turmoil she'd left behind.

The snowmobile slowed as they approached the

island's shore. Max steered the machine to the right of the harbor where the car ferry docked during the summer months. Further east on the shoreline, the Shore View Palace that drew tourists throughout the summer loomed large. Aunt Miriam had told her most places shut down for the winter and asked if she'd be bored. Harper hadn't thought so. Hibernating appealed.

Max glanced back at her. "Welcome to Sanctuary Island."

She took a deep breath, inhaling the crisp, clean air.

He avoided the town center where motorized vehicles were prohibited within its five square blocks. During summer, residents walked or rode bicycles while tourists explored the town in horse-drawn carriages, stopping to visit the shops, galleries, and cafés along the way. During winter, she guessed they skied or walked and maybe pulled little ones or groceries on sleds.

As he guided the snowmobile alongside the perimeter road where the snow was thick, the charming cluster of quaint buildings within the town center beckoned to her, and she winced at a pang of nostalgia for the summers she'd spent here—a lifetime ago.

And then he stopped in front of Aunt Miriam's home, a whimsical, two-story cottage with a steeply pitched roof and colorful shutters. The exterior, painted in vibrant shades of blue and green, had a wraparound porch where wind chimes would dangle and potted plants flourish come the warmer months. Even in winter with icicles thick at its eaves, the house exuded a creative, welcoming charm so typical of her aunt.

While Harper slid off and removed her helmet, the door swung open, and petite Aunt Miriam stepped out, her long cardigan billowing around her like a multicolored cape, her silver-streaked hair reaching to her waist, and her smile radiating warmth.

"Harper! It's wonderful to see you!" Genuine joy trilled her aunt's voice as she hurried down the steps and embraced her.

Harper hugged her tightly, feeling a rush of emotion. "It's great to see you as well, Aunt Miriam. It's been too long."

"Far too long." Her aunt eased back to study her. "Come inside. Let's get you warmed up. It's freezing out here." She peered around Harper. "Max, would you like to come in, too?"

"Thanks for the offer, but I'll bring the bags up and then head off. Another day, perhaps?"

"Sure. You're always welcome. You know that."

As they climbed the porch steps, the eclectic decorations—paintings, sculptures, and intricate wood carvings —all spoke to her aunt's artistic flair. Inside, the house was colorful and cozy, just as Harper remembered. The living room, with its comfortable furniture, soft throws, and a crackling fire, added to the home's warmth.

"And here's Sir Greyson." A sleek dark-gray cat sauntered into the room, eyeing Harper with both curiosity and disdain before rubbing against her leg.

"Well, hello there." She bent down and scratched behind his ears. "Nice to meet you, Sir Greyson."

Aunt Miriam laughed. "He doesn't warm to many people, but it looks like he's taken to you, although don't be surprised if he ignores you. He's a Russian blue, and he has attitude."

"Oh, right." Harper had no idea what a Russian blue was, but she wasn't about to admit it.

Max brought in her bags and set them at the foot of the stairs. "I'll be off now, but if you need anything, just give me a call."

"Thank you. I appreciate it." Toeing off her boots, Harper offered a grateful smile before he left.

As Aunt Miriam led her upstairs and into her room, a sense of belonging she hadn't felt in years surged through her. Her apartment in Toronto was small and functional, nothing like this eclectic house.

"How gorgeous!" Bathed in warm light from a vintage lamp on the bedside table, the room promised to be a cozy sanctuary. The large window offered a picturesque view of the snowy landscape, and floor-length dark-blue drapes framed the scene like a winter painting.

The bed, covered with a thick handmade quilt, looked irresistibly inviting. Its wooden frame, carved with delicate floral patterns, added a touch of rustic charm. A plush overstuffed armchair sat in the corner, draped with a colorful afghan, perfect for curling up with a book.

On the opposite wall, a bookshelf held a mix of novels and art books, along with sketch pads. Above the bed, a framed painting of a vibrant summer day on the island evoked the warm memories she cherished from her childhood.

Touches of Aunt Miriam's artistic flair enlivened the room—a vase of dried wildflowers on the dresser, hand-made ceramic trinkets on the windowsill, and a woven rug underfoot that added a splash of color and warmed the wooden floor. Harper could already imagine spending quiet evenings here, finding solace and inspiration in the peaceful surroundings.

Aunt Miriam stood in the doorway, a gentle smile on her face. "I hope you'll be comfortable here. This house and this room are yours for as long as you want or need."

Harper swallowed hard. "Thank you. It's perfect."

Her aunt stepped forward and took her hands. "You're welcome, dear. It's wonderful to see you again. Now, lunch will be ready soon, and we have so much to catch up on."

After she'd settled into her room, Harper sat with Aunt Miriam at the marble kitchen island, enjoying Norwegian salmon sandwiches with cream cheese and herb dressing and slices of tomato and cucumber.

"These are delightful." Harper mopped her mouth with a napkin.

Her aunt beamed, her smile as warm as her colorful caftan. "I'm glad you like them."

As Harper took another bite, she wondered why Aunt Miriam had never married. A descendant of one of the island's founding families, the Solheims, a family of builders who'd built many of the first homes on the island, she'd grown up on Sanctuary Island. After a career as an art teacher, she now dedicated her life to her art and community projects. She seemed content living on her own with only Sir Greyson for company, but she must get lonely at times. Or perhaps she didn't.

"How was your trip across the ice bridge?"

Harper picked up her mug and cradled it, breathing in the aroma of hot chocolate before taking a sip. "To start with, I was quite anxious, but once we got going, I was in awe. It was amazing. So beautiful."

Aunt Miriam chuckled. "That's the reaction most people have when they first make the trek. It's frightening at first, which is understandable since you're crossing an entire lake on nothing but ice, but once you get past that, you see the beauty of it. God's handiwork. Speaking of which, I'd like you to come to church with me on Sunday. I'm not sure where you stand on God and faith anymore, but I'd love it if you came with me before I head off."

Hmm. Harper hadn't attended church for many years, although she'd been baptized at summer camp when she was fifteen. The glitz and glamor of the dance world had captured her attention, and she'd lost interest in God and church.

But she couldn't deny her aunt. She drew a long breath. "I'd love to go with you."

"Wonderful!" Aunt Miriam clapped like an excited schoolgirl. "Now, I'll let you finish unpacking, and once you're done, I'll take you on a quick tour of the town and get you reacquainted."

Her aunt's enthusiasm warmed Harper. "Sounds great. Thank you. I'll be down as soon as I'm done."

She didn't finish unpacking, giving up about halfway through. With the scenery beckoning through the window, she had to get outside and enjoy it. Unpacking could wait.

The island hadn't changed much over the years, although she didn't recall everything, her fifteen-year-old self having vastly different interests from her adult self. Back then, she was interested in ice cream, boys, and clothes. Not necessarily in that order. Now, she was more interested in the eclectic shops offering knickknacks and books, although most of the shops were closed. But it was nice strolling around town and peering in all the windows, the storefronts knocked clean of the larger icicles that could drip or drop on passersby.

They ambled along East Third Street until they reached the Island Market just outside the nonmotorized area.

The proprietor, a solid man, smiled warmly when they entered. "Miriam! Hello. And who do we have here?"

Aunt Miriam pulled her forward. "This is my great-niece, Harper Mackenzie. She's house-sitting while I go to the mainland."

"Welcome to the island, Harper. It's lovely to meet you." He extended his hand over the counter, flashing his white teeth. "Solomon Jacobs. Owner and manager."

Harper shook his hand and returned his smile. "Thank you. Nice to meet you."

He released her hand. "Now, what can I get you ladies today?"

"Nothing. I was just showing Harper around. The house is stocked, but now she knows where to come if she needs anything."

After a few parting words, Aunt Miriam ushered her away to continue the tour, showing her the post office, the bank, and Cathy's Cupcakes, a charming little bakery with a pink-and-blue awning.

Cupcakes were definitely not on Harper's ballet diet, but she'd indulge while on the island. The sign said the bakery was open until two p.m. on Wednesdays. She glanced at her watch. Fifteen minutes until closing time.

She looped her arm through her aunt's. "Can we go in?"

"Of course." Aunt Miriam hugged her arm. "Cathy's cupcakes are to die for. Let's treat ourselves and buy some to take home."

When the glass door opened and a customer left the shop, Harper breathed in the delicious odor. "They smell divine."

Aunt Miriam winked. "Wait until you taste them."

The bakery was tiny and could only accommodate a few customers at a time. While waiting in line behind a middle-aged woman, Harper read the menu, and her mouth watered.

"What's your favorite, Aunt Miriam?"

"It's hard to beat the red velvet, but I think I'll order the decadent chocolate with a swirl of raspberry frosting today."

"They all sound amazing." Harper chose the classic vanilla topped with delicate lavender icing.

With their cupcakes purchased and safely tucked into a carry case, they left the shop and continued on their way. Aunt Miriam led her past the bookstore. "Whimsical Pages is open year-round. They stock a wonderful range of books, and a book club meets once a week if you're interested."

"I love the idea of book clubs. I've just never had a chance to be part of one," Harper admitted. "I've always been busy with the company."

Aunt Miriam patted her hand. "Working's all well and good, my dear, but there's more to life than work. You need to enjoy the little pleasures as well. Don't wait until you're my age to stop and smell the roses. They might be withered by the time you get to them."

Harper chuckled. "I'll try to remember that." Under her breath, she whispered, "I should have come sooner. Things might have been figured out by now."

Aunt Miriam stopped and faced her.

Harper stilled and swallowed hard. Had Aunt Miriam heard her?

"Harper, I don't believe in pretense. I know you came here for more than helping your old aunt. And that's fine. But if you came here to run away from something, I have to warn you. It might be called Sanctuary Island, but it's not the place to hide. It's a place where you can find healing and rediscover yourself. Nobody leaves here the same as they arrived."

Harper drew a long breath and held her aunt's gaze. "And that's what I want."

"Good." Aunt Miriam's expression softened. "Now I'm going to ask you a question. If you tell me to take a hike, I won't be offended, but as your aunt, I think I have the right to ask what you're running from."

Harper's gaze dropped to her faux-fur-lined snow-covered boots. She loved Aunt Miriam like a mother, but admitting she'd had a relationship with the dance company's director wasn't something she was ready to do. What would her aunt think?

Finally, Harper lifted her gaze. "I need time to clear my head. Things aren't as they used to be, and I'm trying to find my way back."

Her aunt's gaze narrowed. "How so?"

"Well…" Harper released a heavy sigh, her shoulders slumping. "I've lost my passion for ballet."

Aunt Miriam's hazel eyes probed. "But you love dancing. And look how far you've come! You've had an amazing career, and you're still so young." She touched Harper's shoulder. "Has something happened?"

"I…I…" Harper wanted to speak, but the words refused to come. How could she explain? She should've known better, instead of foolishly believing Troy's lies and thinking herself to be in love. It wasn't love—she could see that now. But it didn't make it any easier to admit.

"Hmm...if I had to make a guess, I'd say a man was involved."

Harper's frosty breath puffed out with her gasp. "How did you—"

Her aunt's grip on Harper's shoulder tightened. "My dear, when you've lived as long as I have, you learn a thing or two—or ten—along the way. When I asked the question, heartbreak was written all over your face. I won't ask who he was or what happened. If you want to tell me, I'll always have a listening ear. What I will say is you were right to come here. Sometimes a change of scenery and pace can bring revelations to the things troubling us. I'll be praying the Lord shows you His desires for your life and you find your way during your time here."

Harper's vision blurred as something shifted inside her. She wiped her eyes with the back of her gloved hand. Since summer-camp days, she'd rarely thought of God, but she remembered how loved she'd felt back then.

Could God still love her now, or had she strayed too far for Him to look at her?

And if He loved her, could He help her find her way?

Back home, she snuggled under a warm, fluffy blanket on the porch swing while Aunt Miriam went inside to fetch a hot drink for them both. As the sun dipped low in the sky, it painted the horizon with a palette of soothing, enchanting colors. Streaks of purple clouds, kissed with soft orange, stretched across the teal expanse and reflected from the snowy landscape. The sun's rays, like gentle fingers, reached out one final time before it slipped away to rest for the night.

Tucked away in a dance studio or performing on stage, Harper rarely witnessed a sunset. Aunt Miriam was right. She needed to slow down, enjoy amazing sunsets, and take time to smell the roses. Perhaps in doing so, she'd find herself.

CHAPTER 3

arper woke to sweet birdsong the following morning, something she hadn't experienced since her childhood visits to the island. She lived in a high-rise apartment block in Toronto, closed off from nature. Closed off from a lot of things.

She rolled out of bed and stretched her arms above her head before running her fingers through her pixie-cut hair. It was a new look for her, one she'd decided on right before she left for the island. She liked it. Her reddish-brown hair swept lightly across her forehead, a natural part on the left slicking her hair behind her ear where it tapered at the back. It was slightly matted from sleep, so she fluffed it with her fingers before re-tucking it.

As she stepped into the hall, the aroma of Aunt Miriam's cooking wafted in the air, and her tummy rumbled. How long had it been since someone cooked for her? And this was the third time in less than twenty-four hours her aunt had made a meal for her. Not even her mother had looked after her so well.

She'd always been busy. A woman driven by corporate success whose daughter's aspirations for the stage were considered a frivolous youthful desire she'd hoped she'd grow out of. Harper didn't. And the already wide gap between them only increased as the years went by. She rarely saw her mother now, and her father? After her parents divorced when she was fourteen, he disappeared from her life. Only the sporadic phone call to her mother reminded her she still had one at all.

She slid onto one of the stools at the marble island where Aunt Miriam was cooking the most delectable food. Harper breathed in the enticing aroma. "Do you always cook like this?"

Her aunt chuckled. "Sure do. It's one of the little pleasures of life. I treat myself to good food as often as I can, and we have an abundance here on the island. I work my garden during the warmer months, like most folk do, and preserve as much as I can for the winter months. There's something special about eating food you've grown yourself. You should try it sometime."

Harper winced. "I've never grown anything."

"Well, there's always time to try. Maybe you'll still be here when spring comes, and I can show you."

Harper blinked. Could she stay that long? She hadn't planned to. But she'd planned little about this trip. "I'm not sure I'll be here. But thanks for the invitation."

Aunt Miriam continued to scramble eggs in a pan. A

plate of plump turkey links steamed on the counter beside the stovetop.

Harper nodded to the plate. "May I?"

"Help yourself. I made them for you. It's my parting gift before I leave this morning."

"This morning?" Harper's hand, reaching for the aromatic treasures, stilled. "I thought you weren't leaving until next week."

Aunt Miriam let out a heavy breath. "My sister called and asked me to come sooner. It sounded urgent, so I managed to get a ride to Havensport on the supply plane this morning. I leave in a few hours."

Aunt Hilda was five years older than Aunt Miriam. Their younger brother, Eric, Harper's grandfather, had died before Harper was born. Only Aunt Miriam and Aunt Hilda remained of that generation. Was Aunt Hilda unwell?

Harper asked the question.

"Unfortunately, yes. Although, she's always been a drama queen. She says she doesn't have long to live, but I think it's just an excuse to get me to visit. We do need to make some decisions about her future now that Albert's passed. I'd like her to return to the island, but she wants to stay close to her children. I'm not sure why, since they rarely visit her."

"I haven't seen Aunt Hilda since I was a child. I hope she's not too ill." Harper hesitated, then plucked one sausage link, steeped in maple syrup, from the plate and brought it close enough to sniff. "I've been thinking... I don't know much about my grandparents—your brother and his wife. Mom never talked about them."

Aunt Miriam paused her stirring and tilted her face over her shoulder, her expression softening. "They were good people. Your grandfather was a kind and hard-working man. He adored your grandmother. They returned to the island when they got married, and he worked in the family construction business along with my cousin, Paul."

Harper leaned in. "What happened to them?"

Aunt Miriam sighed. "Your grandfather died of a heart attack when he was only fifty-one, and two years later, your grandmother passed away from cancer. It was a hard time for all of us, especially as your mother didn't come back for their funerals."

Harper lowered the sausage back to the plate. "Why didn't she?"

"There was some bad blood between them when she left the island. They never reconciled, and it broke your grandmother's heart. Your mother couldn't bring herself to return, not even for the funerals."

Harper's eyes welled. "That's so sad."

Her own eyes misty, Aunt Miriam waved toward the window. "They're buried in the island cemetery. Maybe you should visit them while you're here."

"I might just do that."

While her aunt continued cooking, Harper bit into the sausage, the sweet apple and maple-syrup flavors transporting her back to summer camp when things had been so simple.

Aunt Miriam raised a brow as Harper wiped the syrup from her chin with a napkin. "Good?"

"More than good—wonderful. They remind me of summer camp."

"I remember you back then. You were interested in everything, but mostly dance and boys, if I remember rightly."

Harper pointed with the remaining half of her sausage. "Dance and boys. You're absolutely right. There was this one guy, Nate Hawthorn. He was one of the counselors, and I thought he was the dreamiest guy I'd ever met." Her cheeks warmed over her teenage crush. Of course, he wasn't interested in her. She was just one of the campers, and he had a girlfriend. But it hadn't stopped her from dreaming.

Aunt Miriam piled up a serving of scrambled eggs on a slice of sourdough toast and handed her the plate. "Nate Hawthorn, huh? He does tend to garner that response from the ladies. In the eyes of many, he's the island's most eligible bachelor."

Harper blinked. "You mean, he still lives here?"

"Lives here? Oh, my dear, he owns the Sanctuary Outdoor Activities Center. He's an integral part of everything that happens here. Everyone knows him, and everyone loves him and his daughter, Emma." Aunt Miriam's shoulders slumped as she paused in rinsing the eggy pan. "We all mourned when his wife passed away five years ago."

Harper's heart constricted. "I'm so sorry to hear that. It must've been devastating for him."

"I think it still is. He seems lost without her, like part of him died with her. His mother lives on the island and helps with Emma. I'm not sure he'd cope without her." Aunt Miriam glanced at the clock. "Oh my. Look at the time. I must get going. Enjoy your breakfast while I get ready. There's fruit and a pot of tea as well."

She rounded the island and kissed Harper on the top of her head. "I hope you'll keep your promise and attend church on Sunday, even though I won't be with you."

Although the thought of attending church on her own didn't appeal, how could Harper not keep her promise? She squeezed her aunt. "I'll go. Although it won't be the same without you."

Aunt Miriam patted her hand. "You'll be more than fine. The folk will welcome you with open arms."

When she left the room, Sir Greyson appeared around the corner and wound himself around Harper's ankle, purring, as if he already knew it was just going to be him and her for a while.

"You heard your mama's leaving today and realized you're stuck with me. Is that why you're trying to butter me up?"

The cat meowed and looked up at her with his striking green eyes.

"Don't give me that look," Harper chided, pulling a

sausage link from her plate. "I know you didn't come for me. Here, take it." When she tossed him the link, he pounced on it and began devouring it at her feet. "Take it slowly—you don't want to choke. I wouldn't know how to explain that to Aunt Miriam. I can see she spoils you."

The cat licked his lips and continued eating.

"I'm glad you're coming around," Harper muttered, toeing his belly with her foot as she bit into a preserved apricot. It was sweet, just the right complement for the sausage. Without guilt, she bit into another sausage link and tossed a small piece to Sir Greyson who was looking up expectantly.

"Just don't expect treats every day, okay?" She continued her breakfast, Sir Greyson purring at her feet.

NATE and his team were gathered at the center for a final check of their gear before taking the ten guests who'd arrived by charter plane that morning on a bird-watching tour. Seated at his desk in a far corner of the room, he was triple-checking the information the attendees submitted. He liked knowing a little about each person to ensure a good experience, and the last thing he wanted was someone getting injured because he'd overlooked something. While scanning through his on-screen notes, he picked up a conversation between Adam and Chad, two of his team members.

"Have you seen her yet?" Adam asked while checking the emergency kit.

"Who?" Chad lifted his head from the supply bag containing their equipment.

"The girl staying with Miriam Solheim," Adam continued. "I heard she's from Chicago."

Nate stilled but made no visible show of interest while continuing to check his notes, but his ears strained to hear the conversation.

"Toronto," Chad corrected.

"What does it matter where she's from? Have you seen her?" Adam's eyes, bright and eager, gleamed as he questioned Chad.

Nate almost rolled his eyes. What would it be like to be young and carefree again?

Chad nodded. "Yeah. Yesterday. I saw her with Miriam while I was running an errand for my old man, but only in passing."

Adam zipped up the bag. "So, is she pretty?"

"Is that all you care about?" Slight annoyance edged Chad's voice.

"Get off it, Chad. Is she or isn't she pretty? That's all I want to know."

Chad groaned and let out an exasperated breath. "Yes, she's pretty."

"How pretty?"

Chad zipped the bag closed with force, the sound echoing through the room. "Why are you asking? What's pretty to me might not be to you. It'd be better if you saw her for yourself."

"I plan to. It's always good to get some new blood around here. It's hard to find someone when you already know everyone so well."

"Funny, I thought knowing someone for a long time was an asset to a relationship."

"Not if you're me. I'd rather have fun with someone new." Adam closed the emergency kit and pushed to his feet. Chad followed suit, slinging the supply bag over his shoulder.

Harper was the talk of the town. Even after learning she was house-sitting for her aunt, Nate had given her little thought, but hearing his boys talk about her like she was some kind of beauty queen piqued his interest.

He'd been dating Bethany the last time Harper attended summer camp, so he'd paid the teenager little attention and treated her like any other camper. But now that she was here, it'd be interesting to meet up with her again. If he remembered rightly, she'd been baptized at that camp. Was she still walking with the Lord? He could discover that, if nothing else.

"You guys ready?" He closed his screen.

"Yep," the pair replied in unison.

"Good. Stop lollygagging and let's get ready to meet our guests."

The group was due to arrive at nine a.m., and following a quick safety briefing, they'd all depart on snowmobiles for a two-hour bird-watching tour, the main reason people visited the island in winter. The group was staying in the Sanctuary Nature Reserve Cabins overnight. The cabins offered basic but adequate lodgings, and the proprietress, Luana Hodgson, ensured all guests were spoiled, providing them with wholesome meals and roaring fires to stave off the cold.

"Sure thing, boss." The pair sauntered outside, and Nate followed.

Luana's army-like all-terrain vehicle pulled up outside the activities center right at nine o'clock, carrying six men and four women of various ages, all from Detroit and the same multinational company. Their boss had thought this short break would boost their team's lacking morale. Only two of the men had snowmobiled before.

Luana greeted him with a wave. "Nate, here's your group. They're a rowdy bunch." She winked as they piled out of the vehicle. "You might have an interesting morning."

When he eyed the group, he had to agree. He doubted they had any interest in watching birds. An exhilarating ride around the island on snowmobiles would suit them better, with just a spot of bird-watching to satisfy their boss.

Nate and his team briefed the guests on safety protocols and the basics of bird-watching and snowmobiling. After the briefing, they distributed the equipment, and the group mounted their snowmobiles, ready for the adventure.

As they set off, Nate led the way, navigating the snowy

trails with ease. The landscape was a winter wonderland, with fresh powdery snow, thanks to the expected overnight snow dump, frost-covered trees, and snow-capped hills providing a stunning backdrop. Despite their rowdiness, the guests soon seemed captivated by the island's beauty. They stopped at a few key spots, staying still until things resettled and Nate pointed out various species of birds that braved the winter chill without migrating south, their vibrant plumage contrasting with the stark snow.

By the end of the two hours, the group was in high spirits, having enjoyed both the thrill of the ride and the quiet moments of bird-watching. Back at the activities center, Nate and his team helped the guests dismount and gather their belongings.

"Thanks, Nate! That was incredible!" one of the women exclaimed, her cheeks rosy from the cold.

"Glad you enjoyed it," he replied with a smile. "Luana will take you back to the cabins now. Enjoy your stay on the island."

He released a breath and waved as Luana's vehicle trundled off into the distance. As much as he loved leading tours, it was stressful at times, and he often needed to unwind and regroup before tackling the next job.

He poked his head into the building. "Hey, guys. I'm just taking a walk. I'll be back in half an hour or so."

"Right, boss. Enjoy." Chad glanced up but continued unpacking the bags.

Nate took the path along the lake's edge away from the town, where the only sounds were the crunch of snow under his boots and the occasional chirp of a bird. The air, crisp and refreshing, was a perfect antidote to the morning's bustling energy.

As he walked, his thoughts wandered to Harper. She'd been an attractive teenager, full of energy and enthusiasm, and she was a keen dancer, if he remembered rightly.

He didn't notice the female figure ahead until he was almost upon her. Bundled in a warm coat, she was strolling along the path, head down, and seemingly deep in thought.

"Harper?" His voice carried in the stillness.

She looked up, startled, before her eyes widened. "Nate?"

"Yes! Fancy meeting you here. I heard you were back on the island."

Her breath puffed out. "I'm house-sitting for Aunt Miriam for a few weeks."

He shoved his hands deeper into his pockets. "Yeah, that's what I heard."

"She left this morning, so now it's just me and Sir Greyson."

He angled his head. "Her cat?"

She tucked a strand of short hair under her multicolored beanie. A sparkle lit her hazel eyes. "Yes. I'm not quite sure what to make of him yet. Nor he of me."

"I'm sure you'll become the best of friends."

"I hope so." Her voice softened. "So, how are you keeping? Aunt Miriam told me about your wife. I'm so sorry."

"Yeah." He released a heavy sigh. Ran his hand around his neck. Looked away. "Bethany had cancer. Died soon after our daughter was born."

"That's so sad. How are you coping?"

He shrugged and faced her again. "I do the best I can. My mom's a great help, and I have good friends. And my faith." He had to say that because he'd been a camp counselor and she'd expect him to say it. Although he still struggled to understand or even accept why God allowed Bethany to die, he still had faith. Kind of.

"I'm glad you've got support. It must be hard raising a child on your own."

"Yes, but I'd do anything for Emma. She's one of the reasons I'm still here on the island. It's the best place to raise a child."

"I used to love coming here for summer camp. It seems so long ago now." Nostalgia tinged her voice.

He drew a long breath. Yep. It did seem a long time ago. "So, what are you doing with yourself these days?"

She dusted some loose snow off her parka. "I'm a principal dancer for the Royal Canadian Ballet Company."

A sharp breath whistled past his lips. "Wow. That's amazing. Although I'm not surprised. That was all you talked about back then. I'm glad your dream came true."

A female skier approached. Jo Fletcher, who worked at her dad's fishing charter company during the warmer months. He stepped aside to let her pass, lifting his hand to his old school buddy before facing Harper again. "So, besides dancing, what's happening in your life? Are you married? Have any kids?"

"Not married, and I don't have any children. My life's far too busy for all that." She smiled, but it looked forced, and her voice faltered.

He narrowed his eyes and studied her. Something was wrong.

She tightened her scarf and shivered as a blast of icy air gusted across the lake. "So, what about you? What are you doing these days apart from caring for your daughter?"

He folded his arms over his chest and rubbed his arms to stave off the cold. "I run Sanctuary's outdoor activities center. Keeps me busy. I took a group on a bird-watching tour this morning."

"That sounds fun. I wouldn't mind going on a tour while I'm here."

"I'm sure I can organize something."

"That'd be great. Thank you."

"You're most welcome." He ran a hand across his stubbled jaw. "I–I guess you wouldn't want to meet up for a coffee or something?" The words tumbled from his mouth without thought.

She blinked, probably almost as surprised as he was. "Ah, sure. I'd love to."

"Great." Unsure it was great, he smeared out one of his boot prints on the snow. "I'll call you tomorrow to arrange a time."

Her forehead creased. "You don't have my cell."

"But I know Miriam's house number."

"Oh. Okay. I'll look forward to hearing from you. I'd best get going now before I freeze."

He shivered. "Me, too. Until tomorrow."

She gave a warm smile. "Until tomorrow."

He continued his walk, his heart tumbling over itself. Man, she'd grown into a beautiful young woman. He wasn't interested in dating, but there was no harm in having coffee with her, was there?

HARPER GLANCED BACK as Nate walked away, his broad shoulders hunched against the cold. With wavy dark hair and warm brown eyes, he was still handsome, but a sadness about him set him apart. Not surprising. Losing a loved one to cancer would do that to anyone. But the poor man.

She continued walking back toward Aunt Miriam's home, the crisp air nipping her cheeks as summer-camp memories and her teenage crush nipped at her mind.

Nate's coffee invitation was a small gesture, but it felt significant. She'd come to Sanctuary Island to find herself again. Perhaps reconnecting with old friends was part of that journey. Even better if that old friend was her teenage crush. Unless she fell for him again, which wouldn't be hard to do, but would cause heartache if he didn't fall for her. She glanced back again, but only an empty path stretched to an icy lake that blended with the gray sky.

Digging her gloved hands deep in her pockets, she embraced the cold and quickened her pace. Although her future was uncertain, she needed to maintain her fitness, and she reached Aunt Miriam's house in no time at all.

The cottage stood out like a colorful gem against the snowy backdrop, and its quirky charm lifted Harper's lips in a smile as she paused for breath on the porch.

Inside, she removed her boots, parka, beanie, and gloves and slipped on her house shoes. Sir Greyson, perched on the back of the couch, eyed her with a mixture of curiosity and indifference. She scratched behind his ears and headed to the kitchen to make a cup of coffee.

Mug in hand, she settled into the armchair by the fireplace, glad she'd learned young how to start a fire and keep one going, and pulled a soft blanket over her legs. Sir Greyson leapt onto her lap, purring as she stroked his fur. She closed her eyes and forced herself to embrace the peace.

But Nate's question about her life niggled. She'd glossed over the truth, not ready to delve into the pain and disappointment she was fleeing. Because she *was* fleeing. Aunt Miriam's words also niggled... *"But if you came here to run away from something, I have to warn you. It might be called Sanctuary Island, but it's not the place to hide. It's a place where you can find healing and rediscover yourself. Nobody leaves here the same as they arrived."*

A pinprick of hope that the island might help her

figure out her messed-up life pierced through her melancholy.

She had a lot to figure out, but for now, she'd take it one day at a time because that's all she could do.

And she had breathing space because she hadn't told Troy where she'd gone.

AFTER PUTTING EMMA TO BED, Nate stood at his kitchen sink washing the dishes, deep in thought.

What was most interesting about his encounter with Harper was her real reason for being here after all these years. Miriam Solheim could have asked any number of people on the island to mind her cat and keep an eye on her house.

She didn't need a house sitter.

Something had to have happened for Harper to leave the city and return to Sanctuary Island. Now, the counselor in Nate threatened to reemerge.

During his years as a camp counselor, he'd learned to pick up on things with the campers. Some called it a sixth sense. His mother called it discernment. He had a way of knowing what was going on with people just by being around them, and the handy trait served him well on many occasions.

Today was one of them.

Harper needed help. He wasn't sure what kind, but he was sure that she did. Hopefully, he could be instrumental in that. But one thing he remembered about Harper was that she didn't like to feel pressured. She closed herself in. If he wanted to know what was going on with her, then he'd have to take his time and gain her trust until she felt safe enough to confide in him.

The first step was calling her tomorrow morning to arrange coffee as he'd promised. He had an adventure tour scheduled for the morning, so he'd call after that.

With the dishes washed, dried, and put away, he nestled down in his favorite armchair by the fire, put some background music on, and opened his Bible.

CHAPTER 4

*T*he next morning, with the sky gray and her bed cozy and warm, Harper was tempted to sleep all day, but at nine a.m., she forced herself to rise.

Sir Greyson jumped off the bed, stretched, and headed straight for the door. She followed him to the kitchen and gave him a saucer of milk before making herself coffee and toast. Although Aunt Miriam left the pantry fully stocked, Harper felt no inclination to cook anything fancy. In fact, she felt no inclination to do anything much at all.

While nibbling her toast, she wandered through the house. It seemed empty without Aunt Miriam, although her aunt's unique blend of artistry enlivened every corner.

In the library, Harper perused the shelves, picked out a book or two, and tucked them under her arm as she continued wandering.

Cozy armchairs and colorful throws and shelves lined

with books and art supplies hinted at Aunt Miriam's love for creativity and learning. Walls adorned with paintings, their bold colors and intricate details, brought life to each room.

And yet, a weight pressed on Harper's chest as thoughts of Troy kept intruding.

It had all seemed like a dream at first. Being the principal ballerina in one of the most prestigious ballet companies in Canada was a pinnacle she'd worked tirelessly to reach. Meeting Troy, the charismatic and seemingly understanding director, had felt like fate. His keen eye for talent and his ability to pull the best performances from her had blurred the lines between admiration and affection.

Their relationship had started with stolen glances and shared moments during late-night rehearsals. She'd been swept off her feet by his charm, believing every whispered word and promised future. But as time passed, she began to notice the cracks in his façade. The way he interacted with other dancers, the lingering touches, the same lines he'd once used on her.

The blowup at Christmas had been the breaking point. The truth came out in a flurry of accusations and denials, and Harper learned she was just one of many in a string of affairs. The betrayal cut deeper than any physical injury she had ever sustained.

Now, here on Sanctuary Island, the once comforting ballet studio felt like a distant painful memory. Could she ever return? But if she didn't, what would she do? Ballet was her life.

Exploring further, she found herself in a small sunroom at the back of the house. Large windows, curtained outside with a valance of icicles, overlooked the snow-covered garden, letting in the soft winter light. Potted plants, their green leaves a stark contrast to the white landscape, brought extra humidity to the room. A wicker chair with a colorful cushion invited her to sit and read one of the books tucked under her arm.

And then the phone rang, and her heart skipped a beat. It could only be Nate. She'd been trying not to think about the promised phone call, but it had been at the back of her mind all morning. Taking a deep breath, she set her book aside, hurried to the kitchen, and picked the receiver up. "Hello. Harper speaking."

"Harper, it's Nate. How are you?"

His familiar voice brought a smile to her lips. "I'm well, thank you. How about you?"

"I'm good, thanks. I was calling about that coffee. Are you still up for it?"

"Definitely." A flutter jetéd through her tummy.

"Great. It'll have to be next week, though. My schedule's full over the weekend. How about we meet at Eastside Café on Monday morning, about nine o'clock?"

"Perfect. I'll look forward to it."

As she hung up, anticipation churned through her disappointment. It was only Friday. Monday seemed so far away.

She sighed. Other than attending church on Sunday, what could she do to fill her days? She'd never known time to go so slowly. She returned to the sunroom and picked up her book, but her thoughts kept drifting back to her life in Toronto. And Troy.

She hugged her arms around herself and did her best to staunch the tears building in her eyes. But they rolled down her cheeks and onto the book, dampening the pages. She grabbed a tissue from the box on the side table and dabbed her eyes. A pity the pain squeezing her heart couldn't be dealt with so easily.

She had to do something. She couldn't sit here all day feeling sorry for herself. Another walk, perhaps? Aunt Miriam had told her she could use her cross-country skis, but that didn't appeal. Besides, Harper hadn't skied in years and didn't fancy breaking a leg.

Bundled in her warm outdoor clothes, she headed outside, the crisp winter air invigorating as she made her way through the quiet streets. Deicer crystals crunched under her boots, and her breath formed small clouds in the air as she headed down East Third toward Harbor Way.

The harbor, frozen over and devoid of boats, bore little resemblance to the busy harbor she remembered from summer-camp days when the ferry carrying tourists and campers made regular trips to and from the mainland. Nevertheless, she strolled along the deserted jetty. Icy wind tugged at her scarf as she leaned into it. When it grew too strong, she headed back.

She continued along the boardwalk toward the Shore View Palace. The grand hotel, with its Victorian architecture, stood majestic and silent, so different from summer when tourists flocked to visit its numerous restaurants and cafés.

She'd visited the hotel as a child and marveled at its grandeur. She'd wondered if one day she might stay there.

In the distance, the Solheim Lighthouse stood against the snowy backdrop. Named after her grandfather's family, one of the original families on the island, the lighthouse had always been a symbol of guidance and hope. A pang of nostalgia and pride twinged as she gazed at it, feeling a deeper connection to her roots, although she'd never met her grandparents. She'd ask Aunt Miriam more about them while she was here. It'd be nice to know more about her family.

She headed back to Aunt Miriam's house, the walk having calmed her mind. The rest of the afternoon she spent inside, enjoying the warm and comfortable house. She read a few chapters of a novel, played with Sir Greyson, and did some light stretching.

As night fell, she cooked a simple meal of frozen pierogies and hard-boiled eggs and settled into the armchair by the fireplace. The flickering flames cast a gentle glow around the room, and with Sir Greyson curled in her lap, purring softly, she began to relax.

Until her phone rang.

Her heart sank when Troy's name flashed on the screen.

She ignored the phone's insistent ringing. Before she left, she'd told him, in no uncertain words, that it was over between them. Why couldn't he understand that? He didn't own her.

When the phone rang for the third time, she switched it off and put on a movie. Aunt Miriam had a whole wall of DVDs to choose from, but Harper just pulled one out randomly and played it. It turned out to be a good choice.

The movie was a classic, one she'd seen years ago with her mother. As the familiar scenes played out, a small sense of comfort warmed her. *Wild* was a story of resilience and new beginnings, something she desperately needed to believe in right now.

The warm fire crackled in the background, and Harper, wrapped in a cozy blanket, let herself get lost in the narrative. She even managed to push thoughts of Troy to the back of her mind until the credits rolled. Then reality crept back in, and the weight on her chest returned.

She sighed, reaching for the mug of hot chocolate she'd made during a break. Sipping it, she glanced around the room, but then, determined to distract herself further, she decided to explore the attic. Aunt Miriam had always spoken of it as a treasure trove of family history. Climbing the narrow staircase, she pushed open the creaky door, turned on a dim light, and stepped into the musty scent of old books and forgotten trinkets.

Dust motes danced in the light as Harper picked her way through the boxes and crates. She found old photo albums, letters tied with faded ribbons, and vintage clothing hinting at glamorous past lives. Amidst the clutter, an ornate music box caught her eye.

She opened it, and a melancholic tune tinkled into the air. Inside, nestled in the velvet lining, twirled a delicate ballerina figurine. Harper's breath caught in her throat. It was a reminder of her passion, her identity beyond the heartache Troy caused.

With a finger touching the ballerina's dainty bun, she felt a surge of determination. She couldn't let one man's betrayal define her. She had to find a way to reclaim her life and her love for ballet. It wouldn't be easy, but she was ready to start the journey.

As she descended the stairs, music box in one hand and photo albums in the other, she made herself a silent promise. She *would* heal, and she *would* dance again, but she would do it on her terms. Even with the road ahead uncertain, she felt a glimmer of hope for the first time since leaving Troy.

CHAPTER 5

*A*s she stood outside the white clapboard church, discomfort tugged at Harper, trying to draw her back to the safety of her aunt's house. Did she really want to enter this place of worship, despite promising Aunt Miriam she'd attend? With the choices she'd made, she wasn't worthy to enter the house of God. And what would the parishioners think if they knew about her relationship with her boss?

She was about to turn around when a cheerful older woman with silvery-gray hair and large plastic-framed glasses waved her in. "Hello there! Come in before you freeze to death."

Harper let out a heavy breath. She had no choice. She had to go in.

The woman took her hand and drew her into a large entry room where a number of people stood chatting. "You must be Miriam's niece. She told me you'd be coming. I'm Priscilla Holloway, a friend of Miriam's. I promised her I'd look out for you today."

The woman's cheery voice and warm smile put Harper at ease. "Thank you, Mrs. Holloway."

"Oh, pish posh. Mrs. Holloway was my mother-in-law. Call me Priscilla. Follow me. I have a great seat for you up front."

Up front? Harper forced a smile and followed her up the center aisle. Curious stares tracked her as she walked along the rich red carpet toward the front. At first, she didn't dare look back at them, but her curiosity got the better of her.

Smile after smile reflected at her. There were approving nods and some mouthed welcomes. She smiled back, feeling silly to have been nervous to come in. There wasn't a judgmental face amongst them.

Priscilla directed her to a polished wooden pew, second from the front, and then left, promising to catch up again after the service. Harper removed her coat and gloves and placed them on the seat beside her. The old-fashioned church, with its tall stained-glass windows and high roof, was surprisingly warm.

Just when she thought she'd be sitting alone, a family of six arrived. Harper scooted to the end of the pew so they could all fit.

Wearing their Sunday best, the children's hair neatly combed, the girls' braided and the boys' swept back off their faces, they were picture-perfect, ready for the cover of a Christmas greeting card. The mother, a woman who didn't look as old as forty, sat beside her husband, arm linked around his as she whispered something in his ear. He turned in Harper's direction. "Good morning. You must be Miriam's great-niece."

Goodness, did everyone on this island know who she was? She nodded and gave him a smile. "Good morning. Yes, I'm Harper Mackenzie, Miriam's great-niece."

He reached over and extended a hand. "Welcome. I'm Nicholas, and this is my wife, Penny."

Penny smiled as she introduced the children—Sarah, Nicholas Jr., Matthew, and Rebekah, who all said hello in unison. Then she leaned across her husband. "We live down the street from Miriam. If you ever need anything, don't hesitate to drop by."

"Thank you. I appreciate that."

"I'll give you my number after the service," Penny whispered as the piano music quieted and a tall slender dark-haired man wearing a white shirt, dark jacket, and beige slacks walked to the front of the chapel, stepped behind the pulpit, and smiled at the congregation.

"Good morning, everyone. I'm Pastor Jonathon, and it's wonderful to be back on Sanctuary Island for another winter season. Please, join me in prayer as we start the service."

When he bowed his head, Harper automatically followed suit.

"Heavenly Father, we're grateful we can gather in Your house today to honor and worship You and share in the Word together. Bless this service and all who are in attendance. Speak to us in a special way, we pray. In Your Son's precious name. Amen."

"Amen," Harper whispered, then opened her eyes.

"Usually, we start with worship and move into any notices before the sermon. But today, I feel the Lord's leading to do things differently, so we're going to start with the housekeeping."

Harper sat quietly, her hands folded in her lap. The notices meant little to her. She didn't live on the island. It didn't matter that they were planning a spring social and were asking for volunteers—she wouldn't be here in the spring. And the update about the regular pastor who was on extended leave to care for his ailing father meant little to her.

After the announcements, he invited everyone to stand and join together in worship. She didn't know the songs, but she opened her hymnal and tried to join in anyway. The songs rang with messages of hope. God loved her. He was fighting for her, pushing back the darkness.

With so much darkness in her life right now, she needed someone who could drive it away. She needed to see the light at the end of the tunnel.

When the singing concluded, the pastor gave the Bible reading, taken from 1 Peter 5:6–9.

"'Humble yourselves, therefore, under God's mighty hand, that he may lift you up in due time. Cast all your anxiety on him because he cares for you. Be alert and of sober mind. Your enemy the devil prowls around like a roaring lion looking for someone to devour. Resist him, standing firm in the faith, because you know that the family of believers throughout the world is undergoing the same kind of sufferings.'"

He closed the Bible and folded his hands on the pulpit. "It's easy on this lovely island to think we're protected from the issues folk on the mainland deal with day in and day out. But that's not true. Even as believers, we're vulnerable to attacks from the devil, and if we're not care-ful, sin can creep into our lives, often without us being aware."

Harper winced at the truth of that statement. Sin had definitely crept into her life.

The pastor continued. "John 10 verse 10 tells us that the thief comes to steal, and to kill, and to destroy: Jesus came that we might have life, and might have it more abundantly."

In many ways, Harper had led an abundant life. She'd enjoyed fame and fortune, but it wasn't the abundant life Jesus promised. She shifted in her seat as the pastor stepped to the side of the pulpit.

"My question to you today is this: Have you allowed the devil into your life?"

His tone wasn't accusatory. In fact, it was soft and caring, but Harper still felt the sting of accusation. She listened as he continued, but a heavy weight dragged her down, and if she hadn't been sitting in the front, she might have slipped out.

"The important thing is that we confess our sin and turn

to God. He'll never turn us away if we truly repent. Living life apart from Him might seem more exciting, but that's the lie of the devil. The path to abundant life is living God's way. He offers a life filled with hope, meaning, and purpose, and He offers those who believe a clean slate. If you've strayed off the path, it's possible to start again. He'll welcome you back with open arms. If you've never accepted Jesus as your Lord and Savior, there's no time like the present. Both offers are open to you today. The question is… will you accept?"

It couldn't be that simple. Harper shook her head and folded her arms. A clean slate sounded amazing, but how realistic was it? In her world, everything was earned by hard work and determination. God wouldn't wipe her slate clean without requiring more of her than a simple confession of sin.

After the sermon and the final song, she gratefully pocketed Penny's number, smoothed her hair, and smiled at the people lining up to greet her, all blissfully unaware she'd had an affair with her high-profile boss.

AT THE END of the service, Grace Hawthorn stood and clasped her granddaughter's hand. "You were a good girl today, sweetheart. You sat so quietly."

"That's because Daddy promised me a special treat if I did."

Grace tousled Emma's curly hair. She wasn't a fan of

bribery, but whatever Nate promised Emma had made her sit through the service.

Grace also didn't like him working on a Sunday. He had a business to run, she understood that, but she did get concerned about his spiritual well-being. He didn't work every Sunday, but often he seemed to put his work before God. She prayed for him every day because, although he wore a happy face, her maternal instinct told her he was searching for something. He seemed unsettled, lacking direction. She understood. Losing Bethany had all but destroyed him. Thank God for Emma, the light of both their lives.

"Grandma, who's that?"

Grace's gaze followed the direction of Emma's pointed finger, landing on a slight young woman with short hair, seated in the same pew as the Nelsons.

"I think she's the lady minding Miriam's house."

"She's pretty. Can we go and say hello?"

"Of course, we should welcome her." She led Emma across the church to join the short line of those waiting to meet the newcomer, whom Grace remembered from years ago when she came to the summer camps on the island. She'd grown into an attractive woman.

When it was their turn, Grace smiled, stepped forward, and extended her hand. "Hello. I'm Grace Hawthorn, and this is my granddaughter, Emma. You might not remember me, but it's lovely to see you again. Harper, isn't it?"

The young woman's eyes widened. "You're Nate's mother?"

Grace chuckled. "Yes, but don't hold it against me."

"I won't." Harper chuckled, too, and shook Grace's hand.

But then Grace frowned. "You're a famous ballerina now, aren't you?"

"A ballerina!" Emma's face lit as she clapped.

Harper smiled at her warmly. "I am."

"Can you show me some ballerina things? I love dancing!"

"Emma…" Grace made eyes at her. "You can't ask things like that of a stranger."

Emma hung her head. "Yes, Grandma."

Harper waved. "It's okay, Mrs. Hawthorn. I don't mind."

"Oh, please call me Grace."

"Okay. But I don't mind, honestly." Harper leaned forward, lowering her head to Emma's level. "I can show you some ballerina things, but not here. This isn't the place. Maybe another time?"

Emma giggled and dimpled up as Grace slipped her arms around her shoulders.

"That's very nice of you. I appreciate the offer, especially considering you're on holiday."

"I love children," Harper replied.

"That's wonderful." Grace tugged a lock of Emma's hair. "This little munchkin keeps me busy, but I wouldn't have it any other way."

Emma leaned back against her and looked up. "And I wouldn't, either. I love you, Grandma."

Grace bent down and pressed her lips to Emma's head. "I love you, too, sweetheart."

Harper's gaze traveled between them. "Looks like you have a special bond."

"We do." Grace straightened her stance. "Especially with Nate working so much."

"Does... does he normally come to church?" Harper tucked a strand of hair behind her ear.

"He does. When he's not working." Grace bit back her annoyance. There was no need to show it to anyone, especially to this young woman. She glanced at her watch. "I'm really sorry, but we must run. It was nice seeing you again. I hope to see you again soon."

"I'd like that." Something in Harper's expression—longing?—gave Grace pause.

She stopped and squeezed her hand. "If ever you need someone to talk to, my door's always open."

Harper's eyes glistened before she wiped them. Something was definitely going on with her. Grace would add her to her prayer list.

As HARPER WALKED HOME from church, cold numbed her cheeks, but she barely noticed. Since her late teens, when her ballet career began, she'd rarely given any thought to the commitment she'd made to God at summer camp. So yeah, she was one of those the pastor talked about. Someone who'd strayed off the path. The truth was, she'd never really been on it. She'd followed the crowd, got caught up in the emotion. She had no idea what it meant to be a follower of God.

The pastor's words played over in her head. *"If you've strayed off the path, it's possible to start again. He'll welcome you back with open arms."*

But would He if He knew how far she'd strayed?

Unlikely.

But it'd be nice to be wanted by someone other than Troy. The jerk. He'd tried calling her again yesterday, multiple times. She'd switched her phone off and left it off.

At Aunt Miriam's house, she removed her coat and gloves, hanging them neatly by the door before heading to the kitchen. Sir Greyson meowed and curled around her legs.

"I know what you want, but it's too early for dinner. It's not even lunchtime." Bending down, she scooped him up and nuzzled his soft fur. He nuzzled her back, and she gave in. "All right. You can have a treat."

She set him down, opened the cupboard, and found a packet of cat treats before giving him a handful. "There you go. Enjoy. But don't ask for any more, okay?"

He ignored her as he nibbled his way through the treats.

Cats. Once they got what they wanted, they didn't want to know you.

The truth of that statement hit hard. That's what she'd done with God. She'd pleaded with Him to give her a ballet career, and when she had it, she turned her back on Him.

Guilt tightened her chest.

She started the kettle and steeped a cup of herbal tea. Sipping it in the living room, she thought about her life and the choices that led her back to this island. The memories of her past, both good and bad, swirled in her head like the choreography of a chaotic dance.

Her short-lived commitment to God, her relationship with Troy, her beloved career, and her uncertainty of what lay ahead, all weighed heavy.

What a mess she'd made of her life.

She finished her tea, savoring the last warm sip, and then stoked the fire, and watched the flames dance and crackle. Outside, light snow had begun to fall. She could brave the cold and take a walk through the town, maybe grab a coffee if anything was open on a Sunday. Or she could stay in and finish the book she'd started the other day.

But then a book caught her eye. A Bible. She slid it off the shelf and riffled through the pages. Many contained underlined passages. Opening it almost felt like an invasion of privacy, but she returned to her chair and continued flipping.

A heavily underlined passage made her stop.

The LORD is my shepherd; I shall not want. He

maketh me to lie down in green pastures: He leadeth me beside the still waters. He restoreth my soul…

Could God really restore her soul?

As she continued reading, awareness grew—she'd swapped God's unconditional love for the love of a selfish, demanding man.

What a fool she'd been.

She couldn't change the past, but she could choose her future. Troy had told her he'd ruin her career if she walked out on him, and she believed he had the power to do that. He could tarnish her reputation with half-truths and lies, and then no one would offer her an elite position. She'd have to settle for something far below her skill level.

Would that satisfy her?

Was she prepared to give up the career she loved?

What options did she have? She was a ballerina—she had no other skills.

But she couldn't go back to Troy. And while he remained director, she couldn't return to her position.

But wasn't that the coward's way? What right did he have to remove her because she wouldn't sleep with him anymore?

She should report him, but he'd wriggle his way out of any charge. And then, where would that leave her?

She closed Aunt Miriam's Bible and her eyes. "God, if You can hear me, I need Your help. You know how much I love my career, but maybe I need to give it up. I can't go back to Troy. I just can't." Short shaky breaths shuddered through her. She clenched her jaw, fighting against the pressure building behind her eyes and in her throat. But a tear escaped, followed by another and another. She wiped them away, choking back the sob that threatened to erupt, trying to keep her shoulders from trembling.

Crumpling onto the florr, she hugged her knees to her chest and sobbed. Sir Greyson nestled against her, purring as if he sensed her need for comfort. They stayed like that for what felt like an eternity, wrapped in a cocoon of shared solace.

Finally, she pushed to her feet. Something had shifted inside her, because she felt lighter, as if a burden had been lifted, although nothing had outwardly changed. She still had no clear path to follow, and yet she had a sense that God would work things out. Why He'd do that for her, she didn't know, as she felt unworthy of His love.

She filled the rest of the afternoon with a short, brisk walk through the town center despite the light snow falling. A few people were out and about, but all the shops were closed. She found the gazebo and sat under it for a few minutes, letting the quiet surroundings soothe her, before heading back to Aunt Miriam's house where she made a light supper.

Just as she was sitting down to eat, she remembered her coffee date with Nate the following morning.

How had she forgotten?

He was just a friend, but all of a sudden, she had a feeling things might start to improve.

CHAPTER 6

*N*ate stood by the kitchen counter, finishing his morning coffee as Emma rushed to get ready for school. The Monday morning routine was familiar, a comforting rhythm in his predictable life. He watched his daughter, his chest swelling over at how independent she was becoming each day.

He drained his coffee cup and then grabbed his coat and her backpack. "Ready to go, sweetheart?"

She nodded, her curly pigtails bouncing. "All set, Daddy!"

He took her hand, and they walked outside into the crisp winter morning. The air was biting but invigorating. Yesterday, after work, he'd shoveled his walkway and steps so they could move in and out of the house easily.

The short stroll to the school was one of his favorite parts of the day. It was their time to talk and connect before the day's busyness took over.

Now, Emma chattered excitedly. "Daddy, guess what! I met a ballerina at church yesterday!"

Nate raised an eyebrow. "A ballerina? Really? That's cool. What's her name?"

"Harper! She's staying at Ms. Solheim's house. She promised to teach me some ballerina things!" Her eyes sparkled as she attempted a twirl.

He caught her when she stumbled. "Whoa there. You haven't had any lessons yet."

Emma giggled. "I know. Silly me."

He hadn't expected the connection between his daughter and Harper. "What was she like? This ballerina."

Emma began skipping. "She's pretty, and she's really nice."

Nate couldn't agree more. "I'm glad you liked her. Maybe we can arrange for you to see her sometime soon."

"I'd like that!"

They reached the school, and outside the classroom, Nate bent to hug her. "Have a great day, and be good for Mrs. Saunders. I'll see you this afternoon."

"Okay, Daddy!" She kissed his cheek before running off to join her friends.

A lump formed in his throat. What had he done to deserve such a special daughter?

He headed toward the Eastside Café, his mind racing with thoughts of Harper. The anticipation of seeing her brought a strange mix of excitement and nervousness, a feeling he hadn't experienced in a long time.

Not since Bethany. His insides twisted, and he exhaled

a puff of moist air. He'd loved her deeply, and losing her left a void in his heart he wasn't sure could ever be filled. The idea of moving on, of loving someone else, felt like a betrayal to her memory. He'd dedicated himself to raising Emma and running the outdoor activities center, pouring all his energy into those pursuits to avoid confronting his grief.

Now, with Harper back on the island, he wondered… Could he ever let go of Bethany enough to open his heart to someone new? Terrified and intrigued, he shivered in the chill morning air. He loved Bethany too much to ever forget her, but maybe he could find a way to honor her memory while allowing himself to move forward.

The café came into view, and he took a deep breath. Whatever the future held, seeing Harper again was a step in a new direction. And for the first time in a long while, his heart flickered with hope.

Pushing open the cozy café's door, he spotted her at a corner table near the window. She looked up, their gazes connected, and a smile lifted her lips. She gave a small wave, and his heart skipped a beat.

HARPER SETTLED at a corner table in the Eastside Café, its warmth and inviting aroma of fresh-baked goods and brewed coffee providing a comforting contrast to the cold outside. Nursing an empty coffee cup while gazing out the window at the drifting snow, she couldn't staunch a flutter as she waited for Nate.

And then the door opened, and cold air gusted. Stepping in with it, he shook the snow from his coat, stomped it from his boots, and scanned the room. When his gaze landed on her, she raised her hand and offered a shy smile.

He nodded and headed her way.

Man, he was handsome. Although he wore a heavy coat, his broad shoulders told her he was fit, which made sense for the outdoor activities instructor. His sturdy frame gave him a manly aura.

"Sorry I'm late." He removed his coat and hung it on the ladder-back chair before sitting opposite her.

She flicked hair off her forehead. "You're not late." She tapped her watch and grinned. "Maybe a minute."

He chuckled. "I walked Emma to school. I never know how long that's going to take. She told me she met you at church yesterday."

"Yes. We chatted. She's such a sweet girl. And your mother's lovely, too."

"Emma said you promised to show her some ballet moves."

Harper's chest warmed over the little girl's enthusiasm. "I did. She seemed excited to know I was a ballerina."

"She'll love that." He opened his menu. "Would you like something to eat? They have great pastries."

"They smell scrumptious, so yes. But you choose."

He waved to the server. When she came over, he

placed their order. "Two coffees, a blueberry muffin, and a chocolate croissant. Thanks, Winona."

"Coming right up." She jotted down the order and headed to the counter.

He leaned forward and crossed his arms on the table. "So, how are you enjoying your stay on the island so far?"

Harper swallowed hard. She'd never expected to be so close to him, and it was unnerving, almost surreal. He was her teenage crush. What she would have given then to be sitting so close. "It's been… interesting." She chose her words carefully. "I'm using the time to think about my options and figure out what's next for me."

His forehead scrunched. "With your career? You're in the Royal Canadian Ballet Company, aren't you?"

She adjusted the position of her white-gold wristwatch before replying. "Yes, I am. I'm just not sure what the future holds right now. I needed a break to clear my head and reassess my priorities."

"I can understand that." He straightened and ran a hand along his jaw. "Sometimes, a change of scenery is what we need to get perspective."

She traced a finger along the watch band. "That's what I'm hoping for. This island holds a lot of wonderful memories, and it feels like the right place to do some soul-searching."

"Sounds heavy. I'm happy to listen if that would help."

His compassionate gaze and gentle voice invited her to spill her heart, but how could she? He might have been a camp counselor and her teenage crush, but right now, he was just a stranger she'd recently reconnected with, despite their past. She took a deep breath, pushing out the weight on her chest. "Thank you," she said softly. "I appreciate that. It's just… complicated. Ballet's been my whole life, and now I'm not sure where it fits."

He nodded, his gaze never leaving hers. "I get it. Sometimes the things we love the most can also be the things that challenge us the most. But you're strong. I can see it in you."

At his words, a warmth spread through her. Just then, the server—Winona?—returned with their order, breaking the intensity. She set down the coffees, muffin, and croissant with a wink. "Enjoy!"

Nate thanked her and handed Harper the chocolate croissant. "Here you go. Best one in town."

She took a bite, savoring the rich, buttery pastry. "Oh, this is amazing," she said, a bit of chocolate clinging to her lip.

He laughed, reaching over to wipe it away with his thumb. "Told you."

A blush crept up her cheeks at the unexpected intimacy. Clearing her throat, she prepared to steer the conversation to safer ground. "So, how did you end up running the outdoor activities center?"

He leaned back, sipping his coffee. "It's been in our family for several generations. My dad and I ran it before he died, and now I run it on my own with the help of a small staff. It's a way to combine my love for the outdoors with helping others. It's challenging but also rewarding."

"I can see that." Harper sank back on the sturdy chair, genuinely impressed. "Emma must love having you around all the time."

"She does." His expression softened. "She's my world. Everything I do, I do for her."

Envy twinged her at the deep bond between father and daughter. He clearly adored her. "She's lucky to have you."

"Thanks. And I'm lucky to have her. She's a reminder that, even in the darkest times, there's always a light."

They fell into a comfortable silence, each lost in their own thoughts, and a calm she hadn't felt in a long time soothed her. Maybe this island and the people on it were exactly what she needed to find her way again.

As they finished their pastries and coffee, he pointed at her watch. "I hate to cut this short, but I need to get to work."

"Of course. Thanks for the coffee and the chat. I enjoyed both." She picked up her purse and pushed back her chair.

"Me, too. But hey, feel free to stay. You don't need to leave just because I am."

"Oh. Okay. I might do that." It wasn't like she had anywhere else to go. She plopped her purse back on the table as he stood and shrugged into his coat.

"I'll see you around, then." After a warm smile, he spun to leave. Then he paused, turned back, and placed his hand on the table. "If you'd like to drop by the outdoor activities center sometime, you'd be more than welcome. And perhaps we can organize that bird-watching tour."

"I'd like that. Thank you." Hope and possibility began to take root. Maybe the path ahead wasn't as uncertain as she'd thought. Maybe it was leading her exactly where she needed to be.

NATE LEFT THE CAFÉ CONFLICTED. Harper was a gorgeous woman, and he could fall for her if he wasn't careful. But he didn't want to. Bethany was the love of his life, and he couldn't let her go. The men at the Thursday night support group he attended when he could assured him it was common to feel this way, but one day he'd be ready to let go and open his heart to another. He still wasn't sure. Five years later, he wasn't ready.

Besides, Harper had come to the island to figure things out. She didn't come to fall in love. But that didn't mean they couldn't be friends.

He'd pray for her. She must be struggling with something big if it was making her reassess her career.

"Lord, be with Harper. Thank You for bringing her back to the island. Help her to work through her issues, and help her to find the peace and clarity she needs," he murmured under his breath as he walked through the snowy streets, the island's familiar morning routine providing a soothing backdrop.

He pulled his coat tighter against the chill, his breath forming small clouds in the cold air. He passed the closed shops, their windows frosted over and dark. The quiet streets were a stark contrast to the warmth inside the Eastside Café. The only sign of life was the soft glow from the bookstore. The scent of pine from Christmas wreaths still hanging on the doors added a touch of festive cheer to the otherwise still and silent town center.

As he neared the edge of town, Mrs. Thomassen scuffled toward him, her brightly colored scarf fluttering around her neck. Mitchell, her energetic border collie, bounded ahead, practically dragging her along. Seeing who was really in charge during their walks was always amusing, and it seemed that, once again, she was getting the brunt of the exercise. Suppressing a laugh, Nate greeted her with a smile. "Morning, Mrs. Thomassen."

"Morning, Nate!" She returned the gesture, slightly out of breath but cheerful. "Trying to keep up with this rascal as usual."

Nate laughed. "He's got a lot of energy, that's for sure. Stay warm!"

"You, too!" she called back, half walking, half running to keep pace with her dog.

With a wave, Nate continued on his way, feeling lighter from the brief, friendly exchange. He reached the parking lot, mounted his Ski-Doo, and revved the engine. On the quick ride to the outdoor activities center, the fresh air helped clear his mind. By the time he arrived, he felt more grounded.

The center was already abuzz. A group of older schoolchildren was gearing up for a day of adventure, and his team was busy preparing equipment. Nate parked the

Ski-Doo and joined his crew, exchanging greetings and updates on the day's plans.

As he worked, his thoughts kept drifting back to Harper. A strange hope worked its way into his trepidation. Hope that they could build a meaningful friendship and maybe even something more. Trepidation because moving on from Bethany still felt like an insurmountable challenge.

But for now, he had work to do. Focusing on his tasks, he pushed his dilemmas aside. There'd be time later to sort through his feelings. He'd take things one step at a time, trusting that God would guide both him and Harper to where they needed to be.

CHAPTER 7

*a*s the week passed, each day Nate wondered when Harper would drop into the center. He'd been tempted to call and set a specific time, but something stopped him. She might take it the wrong way and consider it a sign he was interested in her. He was. Kind of. But not really.

He huffed as he planted his hands on the counter and addressed the four young men before him. Local lads out for a good time during the offseason with few tourists around. In summer, most of the island's young people worked with their family businesses, serving the thousands of visitors who flocked to the island. This was their chance to enjoy their own island.

"So, fellas, what do you have in mind?"

"We're not sure." Tyler, the oldest of the group, shrugged. At nineteen, he was head of his household, helping his mother care for his three younger siblings. His father, a good man and a fisherman, drowned during a storm when Tyler was ten.

"What are you in the mood for? Thrills? Something more sedate?" Nate waggled his brows. "Something new?" They'd just gotten a set of kites he was eager to test out. The guys might be, too.

"What're you talking about?" one of the other boys asked.

"Snow kiting."

The boy's eyes lit. "Cool. I'm up for that." He looked to the other boys, who nodded.

"I'll grab Adam. He'll get you kitted up and go through the basics with you." Nate waved to his assistant. "Hey, Adam. We've got some kiting enthusiasts."

Adam came around the corner, rubbing his hands together. "Is that so? You beauty."

Nate checked his schedule, which was clear. "I think I'll join you."

But the bell chimed, cutting him off, and Harper entered through the glass door, looking gorgeous in a pink snowsuit. His heart fluttered. Ignoring the reaction, he stepped from behind the counter and greeted her. "Hi. I wondered when you were going to drop by."

She removed her gloves. "I hope I'm not interrupting."

"Not at all. Adam's looking after these guys." Recalling his staff's previous conversation about Harper, Nate cleared his throat and tried to be nonchalant. "So, this is your first visit here. How can I help?"

She pulled her hood back, her tousled hair falling over her forehead before she flicked it away. "I'm not sure. I haven't ventured much beyond the town center this past week, so I thought it might be time to explore further afield."

"Great idea. The island has so much to offer, so several options might interest you." He kept his voice professional as he stepped back behind the counter.

The boys scooted aside to allow Harper space beside them. Nate ignored their curious gazes as he brandished the activity catalog.

"I'll look after the boys," Adam said, although his gaze was on Harper.

Nate gave a grateful nod and a warning look. "Thanks. I'll come out soon."

"No hurry. Take care of the lady." With a final glance at Harper, Adam turned to the boys.

Nate glanced at Harper and swallowed hard. An amused slant tipped her lips. He waited until the group left before he released a breath. "Now, where were we?"

She chuckled. "Looking at my options."

"Oh yes." He opened the catalog and turned it so she could see. "We offer plenty of ways to see the island, which has plenty of places to go. Did you have somewhere in mind?"

"Not really. But I guess I'd like to visit Seven Pines Park. I have a lot of good memories of visiting there during summer camp, especially when we went stargazing."

JULIETTE DUNCAN

He nodded. "It's a great place. Why don't you take a quad bike and ride out to the headland? You can explore the park on your way."

Her eyes widened. "A quad bike?"

"Yeah. They're great if you're not used to riding a snowmobile. Ours are outfitted with specialist snow tires and snow chains. They're single-rider, four-wheeled, and can handle the uneven terrain with ease. They're also a little less powerful than the snowmobiles, so we prefer to use them with beginner riders."

"Great, because I'm definitely that. I only tried riding a quad bike once at summer camp, and I didn't do too well." A shaky laugh jittered loose.

Hmm. Going cross-country alone could be dangerous, especially for a novice. He usually recommended at least two went together for safety, even though he provided walkie-talkies and each quad had GPS tracking. But still, he didn't feel comfortable allowing her to go out there on her own. He made a snap decision.

"I'll go with you. I wouldn't want you out there alone on your first ride."

A large breath escaped her. "Phew. I'd appreciate that. I don't think I'd trust myself on my own. But don't you have the other group to look after?"

"It's okay. Adam can handle them." He straightened and pushed a form in front of her. "There are a few forms for you to sign. The customary waiver and consent forms, confirming your understanding that quads can be dangerous and releasing us from any liability should an accident occur."

She angled her head. "Are you expecting me to have an accident?"

"Definitely not. We ask all our clients to sign them. Insurance requirement."

"It's okay. I was just teasing."

A strange feeling tugged at his chest as their gazes held longer than necessary. He pushed the forms closer and pointed to where she needed to sign.

She leaned over them and began reading. He suppressed a laugh. Most people just signed, never bothering to read the fine print. He liked that she was diligent enough to know what she was signing before doing so.

As she focused on the documents, he couldn't help but study her. Her serious expression, the gentle slope of her cheek down to her narrow jaw. He drew a deep breath and forced himself to look away.

Once the forms were signed and filed, he led her outside to the shed where they stored the quads. Bundled up warmly, he hardly felt the winter wind blowing past them, only the billows of his breath indicated the chill. "We don't keep the quads out," he explained as they neared the shed. "Most people use the Ski-Doos."

She frowned. "Ski-Doos?"

"A snowmobile brand. The one I prefer. I've tried several over the years, and they work best for my needs. They've got better maneuverability and carry a sled on the back. Plus, the shot start makes life a whole lot easier for someone who spends their days out in the middle of nowhere and has to ensure they can carry whatever they may need for any occasion. And on the odd chance there's an emergency, you don't want to take five minutes for an engine to warm up."

Harper blinked, her expression blank as she nodded her agreement.

He'd talked too fast and offered way too much information. But that was the effect she was having on him. He unlocked the shed door. "None of that made any sense to you, did it?"

"Not at all." She laughed. "But I like hearing you talk about it."

"Good. At least I'm not boring you."

"You'd never do that." Her gaze, so full of wonder, disbelief, and something he wasn't sure about, made him feel good. The teenage Harper Mackenzie from summer camp was gone, and in her place was a woman he was slowly getting to know. Her looks and expressions fascinated him. It was as if a veil had been lifted, and he was seeing her for the first time, not as a seasonal teenage camper, but as a woman.

He pulled the shed doors wide and drove the quads out one at a time before turning to lock the shed behind him. He waved her over. "Shall we get started?"

"Sure. What do I need to know?" She moved to stand beside him.

"Well, first you need to get on it. It's just like riding a

bike, only with an engine and enough weight to crush you if you don't drive it properly, so please pay full attention." He held a handlebar with one hand and patted the seat with the other. "Hop on." He wasn't trying to scare her, but he wanted her aware of the realities. Sometimes a little fear kept riders alert and safe.

"Yes, sir." She moved closer, swung her leg over the seat, straddled it, and then grinned.

Man, he was going to get himself in hot water if he wasn't careful.

He chuckled and shook his head.

"What's so funny?"

"Nothing," he replied. "I was just thinking how good you look sitting there."

She smacked his arm. "Don't tease me. I want to know how to ride this thing. Are you going to show me or should I get that other guy?"

The thought of Adam riding with Harper stung, and a strong urge to protect rose inside him. He dismissed it. "Don't worry. I'll be sure you're properly instructed."

"Good. I'm a customer, after all. Which reminds me, what do I owe you? You had me sign the forms, but you haven't told me the price."

He unstrapped the helmet from around the handlebar and turned to her. "Nothing. This one's on me." He slipped the helmet onto her head.

Her hazel eyes peered out from under the visor. "Thank you. You didn't have to do that."

He shrugged. "It's nothing. You're a friend. How can I charge a friend?"

That wasn't true. He charged friends all the time. Everyone on the island was his friend, but with Harper, it seemed different.

He handed her a pair of gloves. "You'll need these, too. Your gloves are okay, but these have a better grip and are heated."

Then he showed her the ropes—what to do in an emergency and how to use the helmet's built-in communication system, glad to have replaced the old helmets with these new models. Made from ultralight carbon fiber and pressurized sound isolation, they were easy to carry and allowed for clear communication between riders. He still kept walkie-talkies onboard, but he hardly used them.

Once sure she could handle herself, he ducked back inside to gather snacks and a thermos of hot chocolate before they set off toward Seven Pines.

HARPER FLEXED her grip on the handlebars, grateful Nate offered to ride with her. She might be a skilled ballerina, but she had little idea when it came to machines. And besides, spending the day with him was a dream come true.

Now, zipping across the snow toward Seven Pines with the sun high in an almost cloudless sky took her breath away. What a winter wonderland! The pristine snow glistened under the sunlight, and the tall pines, dusted with fresh powder, stood majestically against the clear blue sky. The path wound through dense forest and open meadows, the terrain shifting between smooth trails and gentle slopes. Occasionally, they spotted wildlife, a deer darting into the trees or a hawk soaring overhead, adding to the enchantment.

"How're you doing over there?" Nate's voice reverberated in her ear, so close it felt like he was beside her.

"Great! I think I've got the hang of it."

He was a steadfast partner to ride with, always looking ahead for anything that might cause her difficulty and choosing the easier paths that may not have been as fun for him but ensured her safety.

At the headland, they dismounted and ate the snacks Nate produced from a carry bag. He also poured a mug of hot chocolate from a thermos and handed it to her.

"You're spoiling me."

"Not really. I don't want you to freeze."

Good point. It'd be easy to freeze out here, especially when they weren't moving.

"It's strange how different the woods are when they're covered in snow." She bit into a delicious oatmeal cookie. "It's like, in the summer months, there's a warm playful feeling. Now in winter, it's magical. Like seeing *Swan Lake* for the first time. The props, the lights, the dancers perfectly positioned, moving in synchronicity to tell the story—it takes your breath away."

"You love ballet, don't you?" He studied her over his flask.

She blinked. "Well, yes. It's my life."

"But something's happened?"

His perceptiveness drew a heavy breath from her, the chilled mist hissing around her face. Could she tell him the truth? "Yeah. Kind of."

She hoped that would be enough of a response, but he looked at her, waiting.

She sipped her chocolate and stared at the frozen lake. "I made a mistake and got involved with someone I shouldn't have."

His voice softened. "Do you want to tell me about it?"

"No." Her vision blurred, endless white wiping her slate clean. Could she imagine such a future?

"Harper." Nate coaxed her with his gentle tone. "You can trust me."

She swallowed hard, his words breaking her resolve. "I got involved with my director. We were together two years before I discovered I wasn't the only one he was seeing. Heartbroken, I ended it, there and then, but he wouldn't accept it." Her gaze dropped to her gloved hands. "I'm... I'm here because he put me on leave to get my head together. His way of telling me that either I come back and continue our relationship or I kiss my ballet career goodbye."

"He can't do that! Have you reported him?"

"I can't. If I say anything, it'd ruin my career. He has connections, and he'd have no trouble finding a new job anywhere he wanted. I don't have those connections. A dancer who outs their director for having a relationship with them doesn't have much chance of redemption in the industry. I'd have to find an entirely new career."

She held back the tears blurring her eyes and focused on the frozen lake, the endless white slate, waiting for Nate to say something condescending.

But all he said was, "I'm sorry."

She blinked at him. "For what?"

"That you got involved with someone like that. Anyone who'd use their power to coerce you to do something you don't want to do isn't a person you should be with. He doesn't deserve you. If he loved you, he would have taken care of you. He would have looked out for your reputation. Not threatened what you love so he could get what he wanted. Selfish jerk."

Wow. His anger had the strangest effect on her. His words and annoyance with Troy made her feel safe in a way she hadn't felt in a long time. Her voice faltered. "Do you mean that?"

"Of course, I do." His gaze was unwavering. "You're a wonderful, gifted person. You have a kind heart, and no one should treat you like that."

She tried to restrain her feelings. He was only saying these things out of kindness. Nothing more. But the feelings she long harbored for him wouldn't allow it. She wanted him to notice her. To see her as a woman, not just a camper from his past.

But she was being silly, getting caught up in her

teenage crush. He didn't care about her like that, and she shouldn't think about him like that, either. They lived vastly different lives, and in a few weeks, she'd be heading back to hers, like it or not, because what choice did she have?

"Thanks." That was all she could say.

She finished her cookie as the sun dipped lower in the sky. It wasn't late, but the sun set early in winter.

He packed away the flasks. "We should head back, otherwise we'll be riding in the dark."

They rode back to town in silence. She didn't trust herself to speak and risk any of those thoughts leaping out of her mouth and embarrassing her. Nate was easy to confide in, and she could fall for him all over again. But that would be foolish in her situation. Better to keep her distance.

Back at the center, he helped her off the bike. She tried to keep her gaze off him, but she couldn't help herself.

He met her gaze as he removed her helmet, and her heart skipped a beat. She wanted to prolong the moment, but instead, she pulled off the gloves and handed them to him.

He took them and folded his arms. "There's an ice-skating night on Saturday in the town square. The whole island usually attends. It starts at six. It might be something you'd enjoy."

"An ice-skating night? That sounds like fun. Thanks for telling me about it."

"You're welcome." He began rolling one of the quads

back into the shed. "I better get these inside. I'll see you Saturday?"

She nodded. "I'll look forward to it."

As she walked away, a grin bunched up her cold cheeks. She was falling for him whether she wanted to or not.

But was he falling for her, or was he simply being friendly?

CHAPTER 8

$\mathcal{M}$ ulticolored lights strung along the close-set buildings encircling a town square that could have come straight off the Christmas postcards Harper loved growing up. Strings of glittery golden lights extended to the gazebo in its center. A garland swooped along its wooden posts and wrapped its rail base. Three small steps led up to its platform, each one deiced, and showing no trace of the footprints from the band members now gathered beneath it playing a happy tune she couldn't place. With the square so packed, the entire town must've come out for the event, just like Nate said they would.

Snow drifted from the gazebo roof, fragile icicles glistened in the twinkling light, and music danced in the air, along with the enticing aroma of freshly baked goodies and the laughter of the townspeople.

Sighing with contentment, Harper hugged her arms

around herself as she took it all in. She ventured into the midst of the crowd hoping to find him, but the congestion made it hard to determine where he might be. Several booths served everything from cupcakes and desserts to kebabs and popcorn—a little something for everyone.

"Harper!" a familiar voice called from behind an orange-colored booth.

Harper smiled at the woman she'd met at church. "Priscilla, isn't it?"

The woman nodded. "Have you eaten yet?" Without waiting for a response, she opened a recyclable container and held up a pair of tongs.

Harper's breath puffed around her as she pulled her beanie down over her ears. "Not yet."

"Good. Start with these. There are pretzels, onion cakes, potato pancakes, and quark balls—"

"Quark balls?"

"A German snack made from quark cheese, something like cottage cheese or fromage blanc," Priscilla explained. "You make it into a dough, like a doughnut, and then you deep fry it and cover it in powdered sugar. It's wonderful as an afternoon snack, or in this case, an evening one."

"Sounds delicious."

Priscilla continued to load the container. "Have some gingerbread, and you must have some of this butter cake. I made it myself." She finally closed the lid and held the offering out to Harper.

The container felt like a small dumbbell with those goodies packed into it. Harper couldn't imagine eating it all. She normally didn't eat much food containing empty calories, given the nature of ballet and the need to maintain her strength with a good healthy diet, but it all smelled so good. Besides, thanks to Troy, her career was probably over.

She shoved that thought aside. No maudlin thoughts tonight.

"Thanks, Priscilla. How much do I owe you?" She reached into her pocket for her change purse.

"Hush with that talk. You're a guest. It's on the house."

"But—"

"Pish posh." The woman waved her off, beaming. "I won't take any argument. Go and have a good time."

Harper found a seat at one of the tables set up for the evening and joined a group who seemed to know the song the band was playing. Fire crackled in the nearby chiminea, keeping some of the cold at bay. She greeted the group with a friendly nod as she popped a quark ball into her mouth.

A woman with graying blonde hair spoke for the group. "Hi! Welcome to the annual ice-skating party. I'm Candi, and this is my husband, Terry. And these are our friends, Sicilia and Edward Klein. They own a farm and sell produce at the farmers' markets in town during the warmer months."

Talk about getting the lowdown on everyone. When they all smiled at her, they also seemed to be studying her. To ignore the discomfort, she smiled in return. "And I'm Harper."

"We know." Candi waved in the air. "Word travels fast around here. It's nice to finally meet you, though. I was hoping we might run into you tonight. I was getting tired of hearing about you from my neighbor. She thinks she knows everything."

Harper bit into another quark ball. "And who might that be?"

"Mrs. Larsen," Candi replied.

Harper's brow furrowed. Had she met Mrs. Larsen yet? The name wasn't familiar. Still, whoever she was, she seemed to know her. "Well, I hope you can introduce us tonight if she's here."

"She's not. She caught the cold her friend had, and she's at home sick."

"I'm sorry to hear that. I wish her a speedy recovery."

"I'll be sure to tell her. She'll be upset to learn I got to meet you first. She tries to beat me at everything, but I usually get the scoop before she does, much to her annoyance. It's amazing how much people share when they're having their hair done." Candi winked, and Terry rolled his eyes.

Falling into easy conversation, the group discussed life on the island and shared some of its history before delving into the people who'd visited once and loved it so much they'd made their homes here.

"That's how the Fergussons came to live here. After old man Fergusson came for ice fishing with his friend in sixty-four, he decided he didn't want to go back to Manitoba. He married Helen and had seven children. Those are his great-grandchildren playing over there." Candi pointed to a little brunette girl and boy who were no more than three.

After a while, Harper excused herself to investigate more of the festivities. So many booths crowded into the square, and she wanted to see them all. One displayed ornaments, another sold framed photos of the island, and a third offered sleigh rides for couples. The pair must have teamed up, as both booths presented photos of happy couples enjoying a sleigh ride. Harper paused to inspect the pictures. The smiling couples looked happily in love.

She and Troy had few happy memories to share, and love wasn't part of the equation, especially toward the end. A heavy invisible weight crushed her shoulders until she reached the ice rink and the sight of people of all ages skating happily chased her melancholy away.

To no avail, she leaned on the rail and sought out Nate. Weird, because she thought he would have sought her out since he'd extended the invitation.

"Would you like a turn on the ice, miss?" The young man beside her held up a pair of skates. "It's just two dollars a turn. The money's to help Mr. Molenaar get a new roof for his house."

"Sure." After reaching into her pocket for her change purse, she pulled out a ten-dollar bill and handed it to him. "Size seven please and keep the change."

With the skates fitted on her feet, she headed gingerly onto the ice. It'd been years since she'd skated, but skating was like ballet. Kind of. It'd come back once she got started she was sure.

Sliding one foot before the other, she skated around the perimeter until she fell into an easy rhythm. Soon, that rhythm synched with the music and drew her into alignment with the notes, her limbs almost moving of their own accord.

Others made room for her as she skated past them, but enwrapped in the pure joy and freedom of dancing, she barely noticed. It had been so long since she'd felt like this, and she wanted to hold on to it as long as she could. She skated to the center, then swept her leg around before she began spinning. With her arms above her head, reaching for the stars, she closed her eyes and smiled.

"Look at her. Little Miss Independent," Nate said as Emma shimmied her way around the rink, her hand grasping the rail.

Elijah chuckled while sipping his cider. "Hailey was the same when she was that age. Never wanted anyone to help her. Always wanted to do things herself. She's still that way. Only now she's ten."

Nate shook his head. "I don't know how you do it. Four girls. My hands are full with just one."

"Only by the grace of God, I tell you, especially with the younger ones. When Amy gets started and Faye joins her, their voices can cause dogs to howl. But I wouldn't trade them for the world." Elijah glanced at his wife sitting by the coffee stall. "If not for that woman, I don't know where I'd be. She's amazing."

Nate rested his arms on the railing. "A multitalented woman, that's for sure." Not only was she a wife and a mother, but she also looked after the garage's book-keeping.

Elijah sipped his drink. "You can say that again, but speaking of women, I haven't laid eyes on the newcomer. I glimpsed her at church, but I haven't seen her around town. Thought she might be here tonight."

Nate eyed his friend. Something in his tone suggested his question wasn't as simple as it sounded. But then, Nate might be imagining things.

He began to say he hadn't seen her when his gaze was drawn to a figure on the ice. He knew immediately who it was.

"There she is." He pointed with a nod.

Elijah's jaw dropped. "That's Harper? She doesn't look anything like the girl I remember."

"Yeah. She's certainly grown up."

She glided across the ice with the grace and precision of a seasoned dancer, her movements fluid and effortless. Dressed in a fitted white parka and a flowing pink scarf, she could've been a swan on *Swan Lake*, a vision against the backdrop of the twinkling lights. Wispy feathers of hair, slightly tousled from the wind, framed her face as she skated. A serene expression glazed her eyes, and the rare moment of joyous peace seemed to light her from within.

Nate watched, mesmerized by her elegance and the effortless beauty of her movements. She transitioned smoothly from one move to another, her spins and turns drawing the eyes of everyone around her. Her years of ballet training translated beautifully to the ice.

As she skated to the center of the rink, she extended one leg gracefully behind her and spun with her arms lifted high. Her smile was radiant, pure joy emanating from her. A pang twinged his chest, both admiration and something deeper he hadn't allowed himself to feel in a long time.

"Wow," Elijah murmured beside him, breaking Nate's trance. "She's incredible."

Nate nodded, unable to take his focus off her. "Yeah, she is."

You were born for the stage, Harper. Don't let that man rob you of your calling.

BY THE TIME the music stopped, Harper was breathless. At first, she didn't notice the applause, but when she did, her cheeks further flushed. Everyone was looking at her. She dipped her head. She'd completely forgotten where she was.

"Wow, you were something else," the young man said when she went to return the skates.

"Thanks." The sting of embarrassment still tingled along her skin as she sat to remove them.

He waved his hand. "Keep them for the night. You might want to skate again."

"Oh. Okay. Thank you."

"You looked like you were enjoying yourself," a familiar female voice said from behind her.

She turned to Grace standing there holding two coffee cups. Harper glanced behind her seeking Nate, but once again, to no avail. She refocused on the woman. "Grace. Lovely to see you."

"Likewise. I brought you a cup of my famous midnight mocha." Grace offered her a cup, which Harper accepted gratefully. "I thought you might need a drink after that performance, which was marvelous, by the way."

Although exhausted, Harper couldn't be rude to Nate's mother, so she accepted the drink. "Thank you. I appreciate it. It smells delicious."

Grace beamed. "We're selling it at the booth over there."

Harper's gaze followed Grace's pointed hand to the other side of the rink. She squinted. Was that Nate talking with another man? It looked like him, but she couldn't be sure with everyone bundled in jackets, hats, and scarves, making it difficult to differentiate one person from another, although few had his stature.

"Shall we find somewhere to sit? We haven't spoken since we met at church, and it'd be nice to catch up."

Harper held out the cup. "That'd be lovely. But let me take my skates off first."

"Sure. No hurry."

Once Harper had changed back into her cozy Sorel boots, Grace returned the mocha, linked her arm through Harper's, and led her to a group of tables outside The Pearl, an ice cream shop, now closed for the season. The young men occupying the seats rose to make room for them.

"Do they always do that sort of thing?" Harper asked as she took a seat.

Grace frowned. "Do what?"

"Give up their seats."

Grace sipped her drink. "I guess it must seem strange, but here on Sanctuary, young men give up their seats for the elderly, young women, and small children. We call it raising them right. I don't know when simple manners went out the window for most of the world, but here on the island, we encourage respect and kindness."

"I do agree those virtues have vanished in most places. Most people are so self-focused, they forget other people have feelings that should be considered." Like Troy.

Grace set aside her empty cup. "The Bible tells us to love one another, even as Christ loved us. It's a very simple principle that, if applied by all, would create a much more peaceful world."

"You know a lot about the Bible, don't you?"

Grace paused before answering. "Not as much as I

should, but I do try to study it often. It helps me to remember my purpose."

Harper angled her head. "And what's that?"

A warm smile marked Grace's reply. "That's easy. I'm here to build people up."

Harper frowned. Was that all? She waited for the rest of the grand proclamation of purpose, but nothing came. It wasn't to save endangered whales or combat climate change. Simply to build people up?

"I can see that doesn't mean anything to you," Grace continued. "And I understand why. The world makes it seem as if you aren't doing anything of value if you don't have a following on social media. But God doesn't care about your followers. He cares if you're following *Him*."

Harper didn't much care for social media, either, but she was interested in Grace's first statement. When did a person discover their purpose? And how?

Grace must have read her mind. "If you're trying to figure out your place in this world, the first place to go is the Word of God. Find out what He says about you, then you'll discover your identity, and He'll set your feet on the right path to fulfilling His purpose for you."

She made it all sound easy, but was it? Was it as simple as reading a book and discovering your identity? If it was so easy, why didn't more people do it? The answer came to her the moment she thought of it.

Because they want to live life their way.

It was a damning statement, but one she knew to be true. Just look at her situation. She knew the rules of right and wrong, but she'd chosen to take the path she had because being the center of an important man's life felt good.

Grace patted her hand, her gaze gentle. "I didn't mean to preach to you. I hope you didn't take it the wrong way."

Harper swallowed hard. "Not at all. It's given me food for thought."

"Wonderful. If you'd ever like to chat, I'm a good listener."

Harper smiled at the older woman. "Thank you. That's so kind."

"You're welcome, dear." She released Harper's hand. "Now, I wanted to invite you to join some other ladies and me in our winter project. We're making a community quilt to commemorate the people and events that shaped this island."

Harper frowned. "And you're inviting me?"

"Of course. You've played a part on the island with all the summers you spent here, and your mother was born here. And now that you're here with us for the next few weeks, you're making an impact. Every life that touches another makes a difference, no matter how small or seemingly innocuous. It still made an impression, and that's what we want to capture. All those little moments that somehow shaped the lives of the people who live here."

"I'd be honored to help. Just, well, I don't know how to quilt."

Grace's hearty laugh made Harper smile. "Oh, Harper, that's nothing. I can teach you, or one of the other ladies can. It's much simpler than you think. I'm sure you'll catch on in no time. Be at my house at ten on Monday morning." She handed her a small piece of paper. "My address and phone number. Just in case."

"Thank you." Harper tucked it into her pocket.

"Well, I should get back." Grace eased to her feet. "They'll be missing me at the coffee booth. Don't forget now. Monday. Ten o'clock, sharp."

Harper stood, the mocha cup in her hand. "I'll be there. Thanks again for this. It's amazing."

When Grace smiled, she flashed dimples, just like Nate. "It's nothing. I'll be sure to make some on Monday. Enjoy the rest of your evening."

She disappeared into the sea of people just as Nate's tall frame came into view on the ice with Emma beside him.

When he looked up and spotted Harper, he raised his hand and smiled.

A flutter of warmth spread through her chest. She raised her hand in return, a shy smile tugging at her lips.

Emma looked her way and waved enthusiastically before dragging her father to the rail in front of Harper. The little girl's cheeks were flushed. "Hey, Harper. Did you see me skating?"

"I did! You looked like you were having so much fun."

Leaning on the rail, Nate bobbled the pompom on his daughter's stocking cap. "Enjoying the evening?"

"I am. It's an amazing gathering."

He glanced at the cup she was still cradling. "Midnight mocha, huh? My mom's favorite recipe."

"It's delicious." Harper savored another sip. "She brought it over to me after my impromptu performance."

He lowered his hand to his daughter's shoulder. "I saw you. You're very good."

"I didn't mean to be the center of attention. I just lost myself in the music."

"I don't think anyone minded. It was spectacular."

Heat scorched her cheeks. "Thank you."

Emma tugged at her father's sleeve. "Daddy, can Harper skate with us?"

He held up both hands by his chest, as if promising no pressure, his eyes hopeful. "What do you say? Feel like another round on the ice?"

Harper hesitated, then set aside the empty mocha cup. "Sure, why not? Let me put my skates back on."

Soon, she'd laced up her skates and joined the pair on the ice. As Emma skated between her and Nate, a weird thought came to Harper. What would it be like to be a family with this pair? What a strange thought, indeed! She banished it.

After several rounds, Emma was starting to tire. Nate adjusted her stocking cap. "Do you want to find Grandma for a bit?"

Her eager nod jostled the pompom, sending the hat askew again. "Yes. She promised me a treat."

Nate snorted. "That sounds like Grandma. Come on. I'll help you take your skates off."

They all headed for the exit, and he sat Emma down and helped her change her footwear. "Let me know when you want to skate again." He fixed her hat and helped her to her feet.

"I will." She gave him a hug, and then gave Harper one, too, before skipping off to the coffee booth.

Nate gestured to the ice. "Would you like to skate or stay here and watch?"

She wiggled her cold toes in the skates, her frosty breath fogging before her. But the chill invigorated, not depleted her. "Let's skate a bit more. It's been a long time since I've had this much fun."

They glided back onto the rink, the cool air brushing against her face. As they skated side by side, Nate kept a respectful distance, allowing her to enjoy the moment without feeling crowded. Although she wouldn't have minded if he'd held her hand. They moved in comfortable silence for a few laps, enjoying the festive atmosphere and the twinkling lights on this frosted Swan Lake.

After a while, he broke the silence. "So, what's your favorite food?"

Harper laughed, appreciating the lighthearted question. "That's a tough one. As a ballerina, I try to stick to healthy foods, but I have a soft spot for grilled salmon and quinoa salad. And I can never resist a good green smoothie. How about you?"

Nate grinned. "I'm a steak-and-potatoes kind of guy, but I also love a good burger. Have you ever had a Michigan-style coney dog?"

"I can't say that I have. What makes it Michigan style?"

"It's a hot dog topped with a savory meat sauce, mustard, and onions. No beans. It's a must-try. In fact, there's a stand here tonight. Do you want to get one?"

She waved airily, gesturing him to lead the way. "Sure, why not?"

They skated off the ice, changed into their boots, and with their skates tied over their shoulders, headed toward the coney dog stand. The aroma wafted through the air, making her mouth water. As they waited in line, they continued their easy conversation.

"So, what's your favorite thing to do when you're not dancing?" Nate asked.

Harper scrunched her nose. "I'm going to sound boring, but getting lost in a good book is one of my favorite escapes. I also enjoy hiking when I get the chance. It's a great way to clear my mind and stay in shape."

"Emma and I go hiking whenever we can." Nate slid out his wallet as the last couple in front of them accepted their order. "There are some great trails around here."

He then ordered two coney dogs, and they found a table near a toasty chimenea to sit and enjoy their food. Harper took her first bite and savored the combination of flavors.

"This is amazing." She scooped some sauce off her chin. "I can see why you love them."

Nate grinned. "I'm glad you like it. It's one of my guilty pleasures."

As they ate, they chatted about their hobbies and

interests. Harper found herself relaxing even more in his company. There was an easy, natural connection between them that she hadn't expected but welcomed whole-heartedly.

After they finished their dogs, he suggested they stroll around the square to see the various booths and festivities. They wandered through the crowd, stopping occasionally to admire the handmade crafts and decorations for sale.

Harper breathed out. Such a sense of community and warmth permeated the event despite the chill of the evening. "This place is really special." Arms hugged in front of her, she made a slow spin, taking it all in. "I can see why you love living here."

He rubbed his chin, his expression thoughtful. "It is. It's a close-knit community, and people genuinely care about each other. It's a great place to raise Emma."

A pang twinged her chest at his words and her thoughts of the life she'd left behind and her uncertain future. But she pushed it aside and focused on the present.

As they neared the end of their stroll, they found themselves back near the ice rink. The band was playing a slower, more melodic tune, and couples were dancing under the twinkling lights.

Nate patted the skates still strung over her shoulder, his eyes warm and inviting. "Would you like to dance?"

She hesitated, then grabbed the skates, and untied the laces looping them together. "I'd love to."

After swapping their footwear again, they joined the other dancers, moving to the gentle rhythm. They didn't hold hands, but an undeniable connection linked them. As they danced, Harper twirled to a joyful freedom she hadn't experienced in a long time.

When the song ended, they made their way back to the rail, both breathless from the dancing and the laughter. Then Mayor DeBruin announced the event was closing for the evening and thanked everyone for their participation. Nate edged his watch out from under his glove. "It's nine already. How did that happen?"

She shrugged, already untying her skates. The time seemed to have passed so quickly. "I guess this is good night, then."

He shook his head. "Not good night. You're not walking home alone, even this early. I'll walk you."

"There's no need."

"But I insist." His firm tone said he wouldn't be swayed.

She wiggled one foot, then the other, into their cozy faux-fur-lined boots. "Okay, you win."

Grace and Emma found them, and the group started toward home. The pair walked in front. Harper couldn't help but smile at the way Grace listened with interest to Emma's happy chatter. The little girl was fortunate to have a grandmother like her.

And a father like Nate.

A tingle spiraled up Harper's spine. She was falling for

him, and fast. She needed to be careful because she could so easily get hurt if he wasn't falling for her, too. Although, by the way he'd looked at her tonight, she could almost believe he was.

After a minute or so, she frowned at their surroundings. "Aren't we going the wrong way? Miriam's house is on the other side of town, unless I've lost my bearings."

He smiled at her. "We'll see Mom and Emma home safely first, and then I'll walk you home."

She hadn't asked where he and his mother lived. This wasn't good. "But that doesn't make sense. You should just walk your mother and Emma home. I can make it back to Miriam's on my own. I'm sure I can find my way."

He stopped walking and nodded with every word she said. When she finished, he arched a brow. "Are you finished now?"

She rolled her eyes. She hadn't meant it to sound like a dissertation, and really, she'd love nothing more than for him to walk her home. But she wouldn't say so.

"Good. Now, listen to me. This is Sanctuary Island. Elsewhere, men might not have a sense of duty, but here, we do. We walk women to their doors to ensure their safety." He stepped toward her, his six-foot-two frame towering over her five three. "And it doesn't matter how many times we have to walk anywhere. It's about protecting the people we care about."

"Whatever you say," she whispered. Some women would take offense at his chivalry, but not her. To be treated as someone worthy of such care warmed her heart. Troy never cared for her well-being or safety. He merely thought about his own needs.

Nate patted her shoulder. "That's more like it. Now, come on before Mom and Emma leave us behind."

They hurried to catch the pair and continued toward Grace's home on the corner of Superior and West Fourth Streets. Harper noted the way for her visit on Monday.

At his mother's house, he asked if Emma could stay the night. "I'd like to walk Harper home."

"Of course." Grace cast a knowing look in Harper's direction. "Walk her home, and I'll look after Emma."

Nate then bent down and hugged his daughter. "Be good for Grandma, okay? I'll collect you in the morning, and we'll go to church together." He kissed the top of her head and then straightened. "Thanks, Mom."

"You're welcome. Good night, Harper." Grace's soft voice and dimpled smile endeared the woman to Harper even more.

"Good night. And good night, Emma." Harper bobbed the pink pompom on the little girl's hat.

Emma raised a hand in response, but her eyes were barely open as she rocked to and fro against her grandmother. She'd be asleep before Grace had a chance to change her clothes.

The frigid night air danced around Harper as she and Nate walked to Miriam's house. They passed through the town center again, where a few people were still enjoying themselves. They'd pushed some tables together and were laughing heartily by the warmth of a chiminea.

"I guess not everyone subscribes to an early night," she noted.

"Not everyone," Nate replied. "Sometimes you don't have much to go home to, and being with others who are in the same situation makes it easier."

With his words, the cold around her squeezed at her heart. "What kind of situation?"

"Those guys are all single. Some of them because they haven't found the right person, others because they lost the right one. If I didn't have Emma, I might be with them now."

"Really?"

Nate shrugged. "You can't see me as the up-late-with-the-boys type?"

"No. I can't."

He breathed deeply. "Losing someone can change you. It reshapes your entire world, and if you don't have a solid foundation, sometimes you fall and lose yourself. I was fortunate I had Emma and my mom after I lost Bethany. Without them, I would have been really lost."

"You loved her a lot." Harper whispered as if reverencing the memory of the woman who still had a hold on Nate's heart.

And that realization jolted her. She'd be a fool to fall for a man who still loved another. Even if that other was no longer here.

Frosty air puffed around him as he let out the air

captive in his lungs. "Yes, I did. I guess I still do. It's hard, you know. I thought we'd have a lifetime together, but for some reason I still don't understand, it was cut short."

How she longed to reach out and comfort him. But instead, she pressed the toe of her Sorels against a pebble of the road salt keeping the walkway deiced. "I've never known love like that."

But she wanted to, so much.

However, the man she hoped to have it with was walking beside her, telling her of his love for another woman.

His brown eyes gleamed. "I hope you'll find love like that one day."

"Thanks. Me, too."

The conversation tapered off naturally as they continued toward Miriam's house.

When they stepped onto the porch, he faced her, his gaze soft and tender. "You're a very special person, Harper. I don't know if you understand that about your-self, but you are. God gave you so many talents, but you need to figure out what you really want from life. After that performance tonight, I'd hate to see you give up ballet, and you shouldn't have to if that's your passion."

Her chest heaved. How could she tell him she'd will-ingly give up that passion for him?

She closed her eyes, shutting out that temptation. She needed to be loved, but was she once again looking for it in the wrong place? Even if he told her he loved her, which he never would, would it be enough?

Could one man's love fill that need in her life?

"I have loved you with an everlasting love; I have drawn you with unfailing kindness."

Something inside her shifted. Was it God's love she needed more than anything?

Tears burned her eyes. She blinked them back. "Thanks for walking me home." Her voice faltered.

"You're welcome." He smiled, but then his expression sobered. "You're crying."

She raised her chin. "Am not." But then she ducked her head, scraped her boot against the layer of frost on the wooden planking. "I guess I am. I've got a lot to figure out. That's all. Will I see you in church tomorrow?"

"Yes. Emma and I will be there."

"Good. I'll look forward to seeing you there."

"Okay. Good night, Harper."

"Good night, Nate."

As he walked down the snow-covered steps, she breathed in deeply before she went inside and stood behind the door. Her back pressed against it while she listened to his boots crunching in the snow.

Would her crush on him ever go away, or was it something she'd have to live with forever?

When Sir Greyson meowed and wrapped himself around her ankles, she bent and picked him up, nuzzling his soft fur. "I bet you don't have things like this to figure out, do you?"

She wiggled out of her boots and carried him to the living room, but although the central heating was on, the room felt chilly without the fire crackling. "Come on, boy. Let's snuggle up in bed and get warm. Just don't tell Aunt Miriam, okay?"

The cat looked at her as if he knew exactly what she was talking about.

CHAPTER 9

*H*arper woke to light snow pinging against the window and a laden sky mirroring the heaviness in her heart. She lay in bed, the warmth of the blankets offering little comfort against her chilly thoughts. Last evening's exhilaration had faded, replaced by a cloud of depression that pressed down on her like the overcast sky.

She sighed and scowled at the clock. Church was about to start, but the thought of facing the congregation, with its warmth and acceptance, felt overwhelming. She pulled the covers over her head, seeking refuge in the darkness.

As she lay there, her mind wandered back to the night she'd told Troy she thought she was pregnant. The memory was as sharp as the winter wind that had cut through her coat on the walk home with Nate.

"I think I'm pregnant," she'd said, her voice trembling with fear and hope.

His reaction was immediate and cold. "A baby doesn't figure into my future, Harper. If it figures into yours, that's the end of us, and you can kiss your career goodbye as well."

She was dumbfounded. How could the man she thought she loved and whom she thought loved her be so callous? Her dream of having a family, of sharing her life with someone who cared, began to shatter. And when it turned out that she wasn't pregnant or maybe she'd miscarried early on, a profound sadness tinged her relief. It was the catalyst for her decision to leave him.

The ceiling blurred in her vision, the ache in her chest intensifying. She'd thought she could escape the pain by coming to the island, but here she was, just as trapped and hopeless as before. And now, knowing Nate still held Bethany in his heart made everything worse. He was kind, attentive, and everything she wanted, but he wasn't ready to move on. Maybe he never would be.

She drifted in and out of consciousness, her mind a tumult of regrets and what-ifs. Reporting Troy for workplace misconduct or coercive control crossed her mind again, but the fear of her personal life becoming public paralyzed her. She couldn't handle the scrutiny, the judgment.

There was no way out.

The phone ringing startled her awake. Blinking, she sat up and checked the caller ID. Grace.

She scrubbed her face before picking it up.

"Harper, dear, it's Grace. You weren't at church this morning. Are you all right?"

Harper swallowed hard, her voice barely above a whisper. "I'm fine, just... tired."

"I understand." Grace's concern was palpable even through the phone. "We all have days like that. I wanted to remind you about the quilting get-together tomorrow. I hope you can make it."

Harper forced a smile. Although mixing with the townsfolk was the last thing she felt like, how could she say no to Grace? "Thanks for checking on me. I'll be there."

"Wonderful! I'll see you in the morning."

After hanging up, Harper lay back against the pillows, her heart still heavy, yet Grace's thoughtfulness touched her. A short while later, the phone rang again. This time, Nate's name flashed on the screen.

"Hey, Harper. I missed you at church today. Is everything okay?" His caring tone, so like his mother's, tugged at her.

"Yes, I just needed some rest. I'm sorry I didn't make it."

"No need to apologize. I just wanted to check on you. If you need anything, you know where to find me."

"Thank you. I appreciate it."

What a caring duo.

She needed to get outside, breathe in the fresh air, and clear her head of the depression fogging it. Staying in bed all day would achieve nothing, but a walk might lift her spirits.

After dressing warmly, she headed out. As she explored the quiet streets, the deicer crunching under her boots, she breathed in the peaceful solace and exhaled the melancholy. The cold air nipped at her cheeks, reminding her of the sharpness of her emotions. Her breath came out in frosty puffs, each exhale another release of the tension knotted inside her. The island's familiar sights, now blanketed in a pristine layer of snow, brought back memories of happier times, contrasting her current turmoil.

Lost in her thoughts, she almost didn't notice Max Holden until she was nearly upon him. Bundled in a thick coat and scarf, he appeared in her path, pulling her from her reverie. She stopped short, her heart skipping a beat as she looked up into his kind eyes.

"Harper! How are you doing?" His friendly voice shot warmth into the cold surroundings.

She smiled. "I'm doing fine. Just enjoying some fresh air."

"That's great to hear. Is there anything you need? Anything I can help with?"

She shrugged and dug her hands deeper into her pockets. "No. I've got everything I need. But thanks."

He patted her shoulder. "Well, if you ever do need anything, don't hesitate to ask."

"I won't. Thank you."

She continued her walk, her spirits lifted following the brief encounter, each step feeling less burdensome, accompanied by a growing calm. As she wandered through the tranquil island streets, the simple beauty of the winter landscape seeped into her soul. The bare branches of the trees, dusted with snow, stood out starkly against the overcast sky, their intricate patterns like nature's delicate lacework. The quiet, almost hushed atmosphere seemed to cocoon her, offering a silent form of solace.

By the time she returned to Miriam's house, rays of sunshine were peeking through the gray clouds, casting a glow over the snow-covered scene. The light danced on the pristine surface, creating a sparkling effect that lifted her spirits even further. The house, with its quirky charm and welcoming presence, looked almost magical under the shifting light as if offering her a warm embrace. She paused at the doorstep, taking in the scene and allowing peace to wash over her.

Entering the house, she felt renewed hope. The warmth from the fireplace greeted her, and Sir Greyson meowed, winding around her legs as if sensing her improved mood. The once heavy weight on her chest felt lighter, and despite her inner turmoil, the simple acts of kindness and the beauty of her surroundings were starting to heal her wounded heart.

That night, she picked up Miriam's Bible again, finding solace in the words. She read until her eyes grew heavy, the promise of a new day giving her hope.

CHAPTER 10

The following morning, Harper stood on Grace's doorstep, her hand poised to knock, insecurity clawing at her heart. What if she didn't fit in? What if the women didn't like her? She took a deep breath, steeling herself against the anxiety. Just as she was about to turn away, the door swung open, and Grace's warm smile greeted her.

"Harper! Come in, dear. We've been waiting for you."

Given no choice, she stepped inside. The warmth of the home soon enveloped her, both physically and emotionally, and the tenseness in her body eased.

The aroma of fresh-brewed coffee and fresh-baked goods wafted through the air, mingling with the faint, comforting smell of wood and fabric.

Grace led her down the hallway into a room where all kinds of quilting paraphernalia—spools of colorful threads, vibrant fabrics, jars of buttons, and various sewing tools, covered a large table. Around it sat a group of women who all looked up as she and Grace entered.

"Everyone, this is Harper Mackenzie. She's house-sitting for Miriam, but most of you know that already. Harper, meet the ladies of the quilting consortium."

Grace pushed her forward as the ladies offered their greetings.

"Sit over here, Harper." An elderly woman with a head of silver hair and kind blue eyes patted the seat beside her. "I'm Nora, and it's lovely to have your fresh face amongst us."

Harper gave a hesitant smile as she eased onto the seat. "Thank you. It's lovely to be here."

As Grace left the room, Nora introduced every woman by name. With more than a dozen, no way would Harper remember all the names. At least their ages varied, and she wasn't the only one not sporting gray hair. One other member looked to be about her age, Chloe Bennett. Harper smiled at her across the table.

Grace returned with mochas and biscotti. As she dispensed the hot drinks, the women chatted about their experiences on the island and which ones should be included on the quilt. Eventually, she turned to Harper. "You've heard us all talk about our lives here, why don't you share some of your experiences from the summer camps you attended?"

Harper blinked. If Grace knew her son featured in most of her experiences and memories, what would she think?

Nora tapped Harper's wrist. "I'd love to hear as well. Like many others, I used to pray for all the campers each year."

The elderly woman's kind tone drew a reluctant nod from Harper.

"Okay." She inhaled a long breath. "I was ten when I first came to Sanctuary Island, although my mother was born here. She left when she was young. My parents were more than happy for someone else to look after me during the long break, and Aunt Miriam had told them about the camps. So each year until I was sixteen, they sent me. I have so many wonderful memories, it's hard to pinpoint just one, but there was a fishing trip one year.…"

Memories of that trip flooded back as Harper described it to the ladies.

It was a perfect summer day, the kind that etched itself into memory with its golden warmth and clear blue skies. The camp was abuzz over the trip, a highly anticipated event that promised adventure and camaraderie. Harper stood at the edge of the dock, the lap of water against the wooden posts a soothing counterpoint to the chatter.

Nate was there, his easy smile and encouraging words putting everyone at ease. He was a natural leader, his presence a calming influence even amidst the teen exuberance. She couldn't help but admire him, even then.

She'd been paired with other campers in a boat manned by Nate himself. As they pushed off from the dock, the boat cutting through the sparkling water, excitement thrilled her. She'd always loved the water, and being out on the lake with Nate promised to be the pinnacle of her summer experience.

He patiently taught them how to bait their hooks and cast their lines. His hands, strong and capable, guided hers as she struggled with the fishing rod. She could still feel the warmth of his touch, the way his fingers brushed against hers. It was a small moment, but it was the moment her crush on him began.

They spent the day on the water, the sun shining overhead, the laughter echoing across the lake as they caught fish and swapped stories. Nate's laughter was the loudest, his joy infectious. When she caught her first fish, he cheered for her as she reeled it in.

"Nice catch, Harper!" he'd said, his dimpled grin genuine.

The memory was bittersweet now. He'd been such a big part of those summers, and now here she was, sitting in his mother's home, surrounded by these ladies, trying to piece together the fragments of her life.

As she recounted the trip, she kept her voice light, focusing on the fun and the laughter, omitting the deeper feelings she'd harbored for Nate even then.

The women listened, their responses warm and encouraging.

Grace leaned forward, her eyes twinkling. "That sounds like a wonderful memory, Harper. I'm glad you had such a positive experience here."

Harper nodded, her heart a little lighter. "It really was. Those summers were the best times of my life."

Nora patted her hand. "And now you're making new memories with us. We're happy to have you here, Harper. Truly."

Harper smiled, their warm acceptance filling a void she hadn't realized was there. Could she find herself, and her place, amidst the quilt patches, the stories, and the support of these ladies?

And so, the day progressed. Although Harper had no idea what she was doing, for the first time in years, she found herself in an atmosphere free of angst, animosity, and competition. Nothing like the cutthroat dance world she'd left behind.

She chatted with Chloe and learned she was the chef at the Hummingbird and Bluebell Inn. She also taught cooking lessons online.

The day passed with laughter and a few pricked fingers before someone gave her a thimble. Nora showed her the basic stitches, and although Harper struggled at the beginning, by the afternoon, she was enjoying herself.

But the memory of Nate on that trip wouldn't leave her.

Why did she fall for men who didn't return her love?

NATE'S FEELINGS for Harper were growing. When she wasn't at church yesterday, he'd been disappointed. When he walked her home after the ice-skating evening, he'd wanted to hold her hand, and just now, seeing her walk away from Mom's house, his heart had flummoxed. He'd been tempted to run after her, but then, what would he have done?

Was he ready to take the next step with her?

That was the problem. He'd never considered loving anyone but Bethany.

But just one thought of Harper, and his heart responded.

He watched until she turned the corner, and then he went inside, mixed feelings unnerving him.

In the kitchen, Emma greeted him with a cheer. "Daddy!" Seated at the round kitchen table, she was picking off pieces of chocolate cake with her fingers and popping them into her mouth. She gave him a chocolaty grin.

He bent over and kissed the top of her head. "Hey, sweetheart. How was your day?"

"School was fun." A mouthful of cake muffled the words. "And Grandma made cake, and Harper showed me some ballet before she left. Want to see?"

She was off the chair and standing on the floor with her arms raised before he could respond. She turned her feet out and squatted down into a plié. She wobbled a bit, but to him, it was the best plié ever executed.

"Beautiful!" Beaming, he drew her into a hug.

"Harper said she'll teach me more things when she visits Grandma tomorrow."

Nate eyed his mother over the top of Emma's curls. "You invited Harper over again?"

"I did. Is there something wrong with that?"

"No. It's just…" He lowered his voice. "I don't want Emma getting too close to her. She'll leave in a few weeks' time, and I'd hate for Emma to get hurt."

His mother stopped packing dishes away. "Why would she get hurt?"

Nate breathed deeply. Yes, why *would* she get hurt? He gulped. "Because Harper's not going to stay. She has a life in Ontario, and eventually, she'll go back to it. So, there's no point in Emma getting close." How feeble his reasoning sounded.

Sympathy flashed in his mother's eyes as she rubbed his arm. "My darling boy, it's not Emma you're concerned about, is it? You're the one afraid of getting hurt."

"Me?"

"You're afraid of what you're feeling. But there's no need to be. Harper's a lovely young woman, and she has feelings for you, too. I've seen the way she looks at you."

Nate palmed the back of his neck, his shoulders inching up. Was his mother right? And if so, what was he prepared to do about it?

Leaving Grace's house, Harper wandered across town. The women wanted her to contribute her story to the quilt, to share it amongst the many patches of other stories and memories, which was kind of weird, but kind of nice.

It was strange how well she'd fit in amongst people she

barely knew. It was so different here on the island. People were friendlier, more accepting.

Perhaps she'd stay a little longer. It'd give her more time to consider her options. Think things through. But one thought set itself against the idea. Was it worth torturing herself to stay when Nate would never think of her as more than a friend? It was like being at camp all over again, wanting him to see her, and it never happening.

No, she'd leave when Aunt Miriam came back. Return to Toronto and stand up to Troy. He couldn't withhold her job simply because she wouldn't go back to him. That was blackmail, and she'd threaten him with legal action.

But did she really want to go down that path?

By the time she arrived home, the old-fashioned streetlamps were lit, and a light mist had settled over the town. Before she stepped inside, she stood on the porch and looked out. Could she give up this piece of paradise and return to life in the city?

But if she stayed, what would she do? There was no ballet company on the island. And how could she live in such close proximity to Nate?

No, she had to leave.

Sir Greyson was at the door when she entered. After hanging up her coat and wiggling out of her gloves and boots, she picked him up and snuggled him. "Hey, Sir Greyson. Sorry I was away so long."

He purred as she scratched behind his ears, rubbing his head against her palm. She carried him to the kitchen and got out a can of cat food and fed him before making herself a light supper.

She took it into the living room, stoked the fire, and curled up on the couch. Before long, Sir Greyson joined her, purring as he settled on her lap.

Life was so simple being a cat.

CHAPTER 11

The church was having a potluck supper, and Grace had convinced Harper to attend. "Everyone will be there. You must come." Everyone. That meant Nate, too. She'd been avoiding him after realizing he'd never see her as more than a friend. Plus, she'd needed to figure her life out without complicating it further. Although she did miss him.

But Grace was persuasive, and so Harper had agreed to attend. That also meant she needed to take a dish.

She had some saved recipes on her iPad. She found one, a beef and vegetable stew that looked simple enough. She started getting everything together to make it. Aunt Miriam's pantry was well-stocked, but the recipe called for bay leaves and a few other items she didn't have.

She bundled up and headed to the Island Market.

"Harper. Good to see you." Solomon beamed as he set aside the box of canned goods he was unpacking.

"And good to see you, too. I'm making a dish for the potluck tonight and need extra ingredients. Do you have these?" She handed him her list.

"Yes, I have them all. Give me a moment, and I'll pack them for you."

Harper smiled. "Thank you."

"Don't mention it." He began collecting the items. "How are you enjoying your stay? You've been with us a few weeks already, right?"

She patted her arms against a sudden chill. "It's hard to believe I've been here mere weeks. It feels like forever."

He laughed. "That's the nature of the place. It grows on you and quickly feels like home."

"I'm not looking forward to leaving."

He glanced over his shoulder. "And when will that be?"

"When Aunt Miriam returns, which could be any day now."

"Well, we're going to miss you. It's not every day we have a famous ballerina amongst us." He placed the grocery bag on the counter in front of her. "Here you are. That'll be fifteen dollars."

She handed him some bills and offered her thanks before leaving.

A famous ballerina. A shiver ran down her spine, and not just because of the cold. Was that all she was? Hadn't she come to the island to rediscover herself? To find her identity? Was she any closer than when she arrived?

The pastor had talked about identity in Christ in last week's sermon, and she'd pondered it all week. He'd said many people found their identity in their career, allowing it to define them. Others found their identity in financial success and status. Still others found it in relationships, appearance, grades, or reputation.

It was a sobering thought because she could relate to all of those.

He'd gone on to say that the only identity that mattered was how God saw you because all of those other things were temporal and could change without warning. He had that right. Basing your identity on things like wealth, success, and physical appearance was setting yourself up for disappointment. Losing a job unexpectedly could make you doubt your life choices. A single rumor, even if false, could tarnish your reputation. As you age, your appearance changes.

Yep. She'd experienced all of that. She'd even noticed her first gray hair that morning and plucked it out.

The pastor had gone on to say that to understand your identity as a follower of Christ, you needed to understand how God saw you. She recalled his exact words as she continued walking.

"A person's true identity is rooted in what God has done for them. The Bible frequently speaks about how God views those who've received Him as Lord and Savior. In Christ, we're loved, created with a purpose, and uniquely designed. We're not a carbon copy of someone else. God intentionally crafted every detail of our being with immense love.

"We're also chosen. God sent His Son to die in our

place so we could be included in His family, not based on our performance or credentials, but through His intricate plan. Despite our imperfections, Jesus's sacrifice allows us to be forgiven and considered a child of God.

"In God's eyes, if we've accepted what Jesus did for us on the cross and we've repented of our sin, we're fully and forever forgiven. He sees us as new creations, not defined by past mistakes, but made clean and whole in Christ. We can walk in this identity, knowing we're adopted into His family because of what Christ did on our behalf."

And then the pastor looked directly at her as if he knew she needed to hear what he was about to say. "God is unchanging and trustworthy. Finding your identity in Him means you'll never be let down. It's crucial to under-stand that God shouldn't just be an aspect of who you are. Your identity starts with understanding who God is, what He says about Himself, and what He says about you. Your identity can be defined by who God is making you to be in His image."

She'd gone straight home, opened Miriam's Bible, and read passages her great-aunt had underlined, including Psalm 139:13–16:

For you created my inmost being; you knit me together in my mother's womb. I praise you because I am fearfully and wonderfully made; your works are wonderful, I know that full well. My frame was not hidden from you when I was made in the secret place, when I was woven together in the depths of the earth. Your eyes saw my unformed body; all the days ordained for me were written in your book before one of them came to be.

And Romans 5:8:

But God demonstrates his own love for us in this: While we were still sinners, Christ died for us.

And 2 Corinthians 5:17:

Therefore, if anyone is in Christ, the new creation has come: The old has gone, the new is here!

And many others.

She wanted that identity, and although she and God had been talking more of late, something was still missing because she didn't *feel* like a new creation. She still felt like a tarnished woman betrayed by her ex.

She carried the grocery bag home and unpacked it, pushing those thoughts aside for now. The meat had to be tender, and nothing did that as well as slow cooking. She heated the oil and diced the onions, tossing them into the pan to release the most divine aroma. Sir Greyson appeared and curled around her legs, meowing.

"You smell something cooking, and you come running." She tsked at him. "Not this time. This is for the potluck. None for you."

He looked at her unfazed and jumped up onto the stool to watch her preparations. She was just adding the chopped and browned meat to the pot when the door opened, and Aunt Miriam walked in.

"Aunt Miriam!" Harper darted from behind the island to greet her, wrapping her in a huge hug. "I didn't know you were coming back today. When did you get in?"

"Just now. I thought I'd surprise you."

"You certainly did that! Can I get you a hot chocolate or coffee? You look like you could do with some warming up."

"Coffee would be lovely. Thank you, dear." Her aunt smiled as she removed her gloves and set them on the table. "What are you cooking? It smells delicious."

Harper laughed. "Beef stew and vegetables. Or at least it will be once I get it going."

Her aunt eyed the pot. "That's a very large dish for just you."

"I'm making it for the church potluck tonight."

"That's right. I'd forgotten. I'm glad you're going."

Harper angled her head. "Will you come with me?"

Aunt Miriam slid onto a stool and removed her colorful scarf. "I'd love to, but I don't think I'm up for it."

"Oh. You have to come."

She waved Harper off. "It's been a long trip, and I'm looking forward to an early night in my own bed."

Sir Greyson jumped into her lap and meowed.

"And of course, curling up with you, Sir Greyson, my boy." She nuzzled him. "I missed you."

He meowed and lifted his chin as if he knew what she was saying.

"Did you get everything resolved?" Harper filled the kettle.

"Yes, everything was fine in the end. My sister was being overly dramatic as usual. Her condition wasn't as dire as she portrayed, but she insisted I attend all her medical and legal appointments. It all took longer than I expected."

"So, she's not on death's doorstep?" Harper clattered two mugs from the cupboard.

"No. But she's agreed to go into a retirement village once her house is sold."

"That's a good outcome, then."

Aunt Miriam moved aside her scarf when Sir Greyson batted at a loop of loose yarn. "It is. I'd still like her to come back to the island, but she doesn't want to."

Harper poured boiling water into the plunger. "And what about *your* health?"

Aunt Miriam chuckled. "I'm as fit as a fiddle."

Of all the women Harper knew in their seventies, Aunt Miriam was definitely the liveliest and the most out-there with the bright colors she favored. She rarely sat still, and her outlook on life was inspiring. No identity crisis for her.

"I envy you, Aunt Miriam."

Aunt Miriam scrunched her nose. "Why do you say that?"

Harper shrugged as she pushed the plunger down and poured coffee into two mugs—one portraying a dory, the other a lighthouse—before sliding onto a stool and passing the lighthouse mug to her aunt. "Because I do. You live your life so authentically. Nothing fazes or shakes you from your course. You know who you are, and you're comfortable being yourself."

Her aunt rubbed Sir Greyson's head. "I guess you're

right. I chose a long time ago to accept the way God made me and to walk the path He set before me. I don't worry about what people think of me as long as I'm walking with the Lord and showing love and kindness to others."

Harper blinked. "That's amazing. It's so simple."

"That's the truth of it, isn't it, Sir Greyson?" Aunt Miriam winked at the sleepy-eyed cat, her tone conspiratorial. "I don't know why people complicate it. Following the Lord is a choice, one that does mean you're sometimes at odds with the world, but it's the only choice if you want to be truly free."

The words bounced around inside Harper. *Truly free... Choice...*

Almost exactly what Grace had told her earlier that week after the other ladies had left the quilting session and what the pastor had said in his sermon. Harper's life was at a crossroads. Now, she had to make a choice, not only regarding her career but also her identity.

Did she believe what God said about her or not?

She swallowed hard and met her aunt's gaze. "I'm still working on that."

"I urge you to take it seriously. No one knows how much time they have left on this earth. Things can change in an instant, but you know that. I don't want to be morbid, but it's the biggest decision you'll ever make. Bigger than where you're going to live, what you're going to do career wise, or who you'll marry." Her aunt waggled a finger. "Speaking of that, have you seen much of Nate while I've been away?"

Harper's eyes popped. In one breath, Aunt Miriam mentioned both marriage and Nate. Now, that was crazy. Harper blew out a breath and sipped her coffee. "I've seen him a bit."

"Good. I'm glad. I had a feeling you might have gotten together."

"We haven't gotten together!"

Her aunt's grin crinkled up her cheeks. "Not yet. Anyway, my bed's calling. Have a lovely potluck tonight."

Left alone, Harper stared out the window, her aunt's words echoing. Life's biggest decisions were often the hardest to make. And here she was, standing at a crossroads, uncertain of which path to take.

The mist outside had lifted, revealing the snow-draped landscape in a soft light. She could see the faint outlines of the town's buildings, each with its own story, its own place in this small community.

She sighed and turned away from the window, her thoughts drifting back to the evening ahead. The church potluck was an opportunity to immerse herself further into the island's life, to connect with the people who had welcomed her so warmly. Yet, a part of her felt like an outsider, a visitor who would soon leave now that Aunt Miriam had returned.

But leave and go where remained the question. She'd blocked Troy's number and hadn't spoken to him since she'd left. She needed to go back to Toronto at some stage because all her belongings were there, and there was no point paying rent if she wasn't living in her apartment.

But could she return to her position in the dance company?

Troy would make it almost impossible.

With a heavy sigh, she checked the clock. There was still some time before she needed to head out. Perhaps she could visit the cemetery and find her grandparents' graves.

She grabbed her coat and gloves and headed outside.

The crisp air nipped at her cheeks as she walked the half-mile or so to the cemetery in the center of the island. Aunt Miriam had given her simple directions, but the place seemed to call to her, guiding her steps. The narrow road was clear of snow, but on either side, white stretched forever. She came upon the cemetery, and through a metal arch marking the entrance, rows of gravestones stood like silent sentinels, each with its own story. She slowed, reading names and dates where the snowdrifts allowed, wondering about the lives they represented. She found her grandparents' graves near an old oak tree, their headstones simple but lovingly maintained.

She knelt between them, her fingers tracing the engraved names. "Eric and Helen Solheim," she whispered. "I wish I had known you."

A gentle breeze whistled through the bare trees, and she closed her eyes, letting the peace wash over her. She felt a connection here, a sense of belonging that had eluded her for so long.

"I'm sorry Mom never made peace with you," she said. "But I'm here now, and I hope that counts for something."

Her boots protecting her from the snow, she crouched there for a long time, talking to her grandparents, sharing her hopes and fears. By the time she stood to leave, she felt lighter, as if some of her burdens had been lifted. She glanced back one last time before heading back to town. Maybe, for the first time in a long while, she was where she needed to be.

Back home, after inspecting the stew through the lid, she grabbed an apple, picked up the photo albums she'd found in the attic, and settled onto the couch. Flipping through the pages, she discovered pictures of her grandparents, young and vibrant, full of life and love. She smiled at a photo of them dancing at a summer picnic, a glimpse of the happiness they'd shared. It was such a pity she'd never met them. Immersed in the photos, she almost forgot the potluck until the timer went off. She set the albums aside and hurried to get ready.

CHAPTER 12

*N*ate's breath puffed into the chilly air as he walked toward the church, the road salt crunching beneath his boots. Beside him, Emma skipped along, her curly hair bouncing with each step as her mittened hands clutched a container of cheese biscuits. On his other side, his mother picked her way along, a bag brimming with assorted baked treats swinging from her arm. Nate had a duffel bag slung over his shoulder, packed with heavier items. The church potluck was a big event, and as always, his mother had gone all out.

"Be careful, Nate. I don't want anything to spill," she cautioned, her breath visible in the cold air.

"I packed it well, Mom. You don't have to worry. Besides, you used spill-proof containers. Nothing should leak."

"I just feel we should have used the sled and pulled it. It might have been safer."

He stifled a groan. He loved his mother, but sometimes she fussed too much. "I'm fine carrying the bag, really."

She let out a sigh. "Fine. But next time, we'll use the sled."

He shrugged. It was easier to agree than argue.

They reached the church, its modest white-painted exterior blending into the snowy landscape. Soon they entered the hall where the potluck was being held, a wave of warmth and the mouthwatering aroma of home-cooked dishes greeted them, along with chatter and laughter.

He'd snacked while helping his mother with her preparations, but he hadn't had a full meal all day. It was also hair-washing day for Emma, and that always took time since her hair was thick and curly. When he washed it all at once, he often ended up tangling it more than anything. He now washed it in sections and used smoothing products before braiding it, a skill he still struggled with, but was determined to master.

His gaze landed on Harper as if his eyes were drawn to her. Man, she was gorgeous. Her emerald-green jumpsuit highlighted her fair skin and reddish-brown hair and showed off her lithe figure, but her smile captivated him the most. She was working with the other ladies to set the table for dinner, and she didn't see him or his mother and daughter enter, which gave him a chance to observe her.

She moved gracefully, like the ballerina she was, her every gesture delicate, her body in constant flow as she set out one dish after another.

Emma tugged at his sleeve. "Daddy, there's Harper."

"I think your father already saw her," his mother whispered, trying to hide a grin—and failing dismally.

Before Nate could say anything, Emma scooted off in Harper's direction. He followed her, and her small voice caught everyone's attention with her exuberant greeting.

Skidding to a halt in front of Harper, he grabbed Emma's shoulder. "Sorry. She's a bit excited tonight."

"I can see that." Harper bent to focus on his daughter. "Emma, you brought something to share?"

"I helped Grandma make cheese biscuits."

Nate straightened behind his daughter. "Good evening, ladies. We come bearing food."

He eyed the lineup. Amused gazes darted between him and Harper. If only the floor would open up and swallow him.

Priscilla Holloway stepped forward and held out her hand. "You're just in time. Let me take your bag."

He handed it over. Then his mother waved him off. "Why don't you chat with Harper? I can look after Emma."

Nate blinked. "Mom!"

"Off you go." She steered Emma toward a group of children from school.

Harper quirked a brow.

Nate dug his hands deep into his pockets, his shoulders inching up. "Sorry about that."

She ducked her head and tucked some of that reddish-brown hair behind her ear. "It's okay. How are you doing?"

"Good. How are you? I haven't seen you in a while." He groaned. Such small talk. But he couldn't speak the words he wanted to. They just wouldn't come.

"The quilt project's been keeping me busy."

Something warmed inside him as he pictured her at his mother's table alongside the quilting ladies, although he couldn't quite see her as the sewing type. "You're enjoying it?"

"I am. I didn't think I would, but it's been quite ther-apeutic."

"Oh?" Sewing could be therapeutic? Like fishing, perhaps. "In what way?"

Before she could answer, Pastor Jonathon stood and cleared his throat. "Everyone! We're ready to start. If you'd kindly take your seats before we say grace."

Nate raised a hand. "Do you have a seat?"

She fingered a chunk of her hair, her fingers gliding down it, then losing it as if she'd expected it to keep going. "Not yet."

"Sit with us. Emma would love that."

Her brows winged up, and she blinked. "Oh. Okay."

They found a table near the center. Emma sat beside him, chatting nonstop to Harper who sat opposite. Harper listened intently, nodding and smiling, but not getting any chance to reply until Pastor Jonathon asked for quiet.

Nate squeezed Emma's hand and put his finger to his mouth.

She giggled and stopped talking as Pastor Jonathon

welcomed everyone to the gathering. "It's wonderful to see so many people here. Thank you all for coming and for bringing this delicious food. Let's bow our heads and give thanks."

Before Nate lowered his head, his gaze met Harper's, and a smile lifted his lips.

Pastor Jonathon's deep voice resonated through the room. "Lord God, we pause to give You thanks on this very chilly evening. Thank You that the fellowship in this room is warm. We thank You for friends, family, and this lovingly prepared food. Bless us this evening as we share together. In the precious name of our Lord Jesus Christ. Amen."

As the amens echoed, Emma tugged at Nate's sleeve, her eyes wide. "Can we start eating now?"

He pressed a finger on her upturned nose, causing her to scrunch it and wriggle away. "Yes, but we'll have to take our turn."

The room bustled as people lined up at the long buffet tables. The tantalizing smells made Nate's stomach rumble again. He guided Emma and Harper toward the end of the line, where they waited, exchanging small talk with others.

"So, what's your favorite dish at these potlucks?" Harper asked as they inched forward.

Hmm. Good question. "I have to say, my mom's macaroni and cheese is a strong contender. But there's also Mrs. Larsen's apple pie. It's legendary."

Harper smiled. "I'll have to try both."

He leaned closer and lowered his voice. "At least we don't have Gail Olsen's tamale pie in the mix. She takes it to the Lutheran church's potluck. I hear it's awful, but no one's brave enough to tell her."

"Someone should. The poor lady."

He shrugged. "Yeah, well. She's the pastor's wife." That wasn't the full story, but Harper didn't need to hear it right now.

They reached the front of the line, and Nate helped Emma fill her plate with a bit of everything. He pointed out the macaroni and cheese dish to Harper who added a portion to her plate. She also pointed out the stew she'd made.

He looked at her. "You made that?"

"Don't sound so surprised!"

Idiot. "I'm sorry. I didn't mean it to come out like that. It looks great. I just didn't know you cooked."

She grinned. "I don't."

"Well, from someone who doesn't cook, it looks like a tasty hearty stew." He ladled a heaping spoonful onto his plate.

She chuckled. "I hope it tastes better than Mrs. Olsen's tamale pie. Better give me some, but just a small serving."

Once they had their food, they returned to their table and settled in.

Emma dug into her cheese biscuits. "Harper, try one of these. Grandma and I made them."

Harper took a biscuit and nibbled it, her eyes widening. "It's delicious! You and your grandma make a great team."

Emma beamed, and a warm contentment washed over him as he gazed at the woman opposite. She fit in effortlessly, her laughter blending with the others in the room.

And his daughter adored her.

But since the ice-skating night, they'd barely spoken, and as far as he knew, she hadn't decided what she was doing with her job, with Troy, with God.

But as he looked at her, he knew he was falling for her....

After dessert, the children played while the adults chatted. Emma joined a group in a corner, leaving Nate and Harper alone at the table, his mother having left to chat with some friends.

"I can't believe how quickly Emma's growing up." He watched his daughter, unsure whether the words were a lament or boast.

Something tender glazed Harper's gaze. "She's a wonderful little girl. You've done a great job with her."

"Thanks. It's not always easy, but she makes it worth it." He raised his coffee cup, both hands locked around it. "Have you decided what you're doing yet?"

She sighed and toyed with a saltshaker. "Not yet. Aunt Miriam came home today, so there's no need for me to stay any longer."

"But you might?"

She rubbed her arms as if chasing away a chill. "I don't

know what I want. I thought I'd have clarity by now, but I'm still trying to figure things out." A shiver seemed to go over her, visible in the slightest tremor. "I'm not ready to leave, but if I want any chance of keeping my job, I need to go home and face Troy."

After a long pause, she lifted her gaze, her eyes clouded.

He wanted to reach out and squeeze her hand. Offer comfort.

But he didn't. Instead, he sipped his coffee and lowered the mug. "Figuring out what you want is a process, but if you're trusting God, He *will* lead you."

She breathed out heavily. "I'm still working on that."

"I think we all are, if we're honest."

Emma's happy laughter interrupted the moment, and they both turned to watch her.

THE LONGER HARPER chatted with Nate, the more she knew what she wanted—him. But was there room in his heart for her?

He still loved his late wife. Harper couldn't play second fiddle again.

Besides, she needed to find her own identity, not in a man, even if that man was Nate Hawthorn.

When the evening wound down, people started packing up their dishes and tidying the hall. The warmth and camaraderie had left her feeling lighter, but the uncertainty about her future still weighed on her.

As she helped clear the table, Nate hovered, looking uncomfortable before he cleared his throat. "Harper, can I walk you home?"

She blinked, her heart thudding at the vulnerability in his eyes. Perhaps he did feel for her, after all. "I'd love that. Thank you."

With the last of the cleanup done, she shrugged into her coat, slipped on her beanie and gloves, and stepped out into the crisp night air alongside Nate, Emma, and Grace. A light snow was falling, and memories of a similar walk not so long ago surfaced. That magical night when she'd danced on ice and thought Nate cared for her.

Followed by a tumble of confusion and soul-searching.

Had anything changed since then?

The road salt crunched under their boots as they walked through the quiet streets, their steps in sync. She tried not to romanticize the fact, but each time their steps matched, she couldn't help thinking what-if. What if he did feel for her as she felt for him?

As before, Nate escorted his mother and Emma home first, and Grace insisted that Emma sleep overnight. "I'll take her to church in the morning. You two spend some time together."

It wasn't half obvious that Grace was matchmaking. Harper shared an amused look with Nate.

"Okay, thanks, Mom." At their gate, he bent and

hugged his daughter. "You be good for Grandma, and I'll see you in the morning. Okay?"

"Okay. I love you, Daddy."

"I love you, too, sweetheart."

When he released her, she stepped in front of Harper, placed her head on Harper's stomach, and slipped her arms around her hips.

Harper's heart melted as she drew Emma close. The warmth of the little girl's embrace seeped into her, soothing some of the anxiety gnawing at her. She stroked Emma's hair, affection and protectiveness surging through her.

The child's innocence and unconditional love made Harper's doubts and fears less overwhelming, at least for the moment. As she pulled away, longing mixed with Harper's gratitude. The simple act of being held by the little girl filled a void she hadn't realized was so deep.

"Good night, Emma," she whispered, her voice choking. "Sleep well."

Emma beamed up at her. "Good night, Harper."

When Grace and Emma left to go inside, Harper and Nate resumed their walk to Miriam's house.

The crisp night air felt invigorating, each breath sharp and clear. The town was quiet, the snow muffling their footsteps and creating a serene, almost magical atmosphere. Harper's thoughts drifted back to the potluck, the warmth and laughter and his vulnerability when he asked to walk her home. Her heart tripped when their gazes met, his eyes reflecting the same uncertain hope she felt.

They continued with small talk, discussing the potluck and the dishes they'd tried. As they neared Miriam's home, the conversation tapered off, leaving a comfortable silence.

At the house, Nate walked with her up the steps to the porch. She paused, her hand on the doorknob, her eyes searching his.

"Would... would you like to come in for a coffee?" Despite the fluttering in her chest, her voice was steady.

He breathed deeply before smiling. "I'd like that."

He followed her into the house, her stomach flipping as he helped her out of her coat. She took his and hung both in the hall closet while he lined their boots on the drip tray before she led him into the kitchen. Sir Greyson appeared around the corner with a meow.

"Hi, Sir Greyson. Why aren't you with your mommy?"

He ran toward her and rubbed against her ankle.

"He seems to like you." Nate slipped onto one of the barstools as she started the percolator.

She scooped up the fluffy cat and hugged him. "We have an understanding. He's a good cat if he gives you a chance. Would you like to hold him?" She held the cat out, but he squirmed out of her hands and scurried away.

"I guess that's a no." Nate laughed.

She rolled her eyes. "I'm sorry."

"He doesn't know me. It's fine."

Their gazes lingered on one another, Harper's heart racing as she lost herself in those brown depths.

She quickly turned to the percolator—the coffee was almost brewed. She stood nearby to wait, trying her best to calm her heart. If she looked at Nate again, she might lose it for good.

They drank their coffee and engaged in small talk. She offered some butter cookies, but they were both full after the potluck, so the container remained untouched.

Once they finished, she walked him to the door, although she didn't want him to leave so soon. But if he'd stayed longer, she might have said things that could ruin their friendship, and she couldn't risk that.

He paused in the entryway, looking so handsome her heart hurt. "Thanks for the coffee."

She swallowed hard. "You're welcome."

Moments passed.

He stepped toward her. "Can I get a hug?"

She met his gaze, her pulse thrumming, before she leaned in and slipped her arms around him. Closing her eyes, she lost herself in his strong arms, his warm chest, and his woodsy cologne. If she could, she'd stay there forever.

She loved him.

But did he love her back?

~

THE MOMENT HARPER stepped into his arms, Nate knew he never wanted her to leave them. She was warm, like home, and fit against him like a snug sleeping bag. He hadn't intended the hug to become what it did, but leaving Miriam's home, he knew things would never be the same. He could no longer deny his feelings.

Idiot. Why hadn't he said something instead of walking away? Sure, he said he'd see her at church the next day, but he'd let the moment slip.

Was fear still holding him back?

As he trudged home, confusion and longing swirled like the snow flurries falling from the sky. Although quiet embraced him, it didn't calm his restless heart. The fresh snow softened his steps, each clomp echoing his unresolved feelings. At home, he stomped the snow off his boots, unlocked the door, and stepped into the silence, feeling the weight of emptiness without Emma's cheerful chatter.

He toed off his boots and shrugged off his coat and set it aside. His gaze drifted to a picture on the mantel. Bethany, her bright smile captured forever in that moment of happiness, looked back at him. He picked up the frame and traced the outline of her face. Memories flooded back—their first meeting on the island, the way her laughter warmed something deep inside him, their shared dreams and hopes. They'd fallen in love amidst the island's beauty, their connection as natural as the changing seasons.

His throat tightened when he recalled the joy of

discovering they were expecting Emma, a joy overshadowed by Bethany's illness. The cruel twist of fate that had taken her away so soon after Emma's birth still haunted him. He well remembered her final days, his helplessness while she slipped away, his promise to love and protect their daughter.

A single tear escaped, followed by another. He clutched the frame to his chest. The ache of loss remained as fresh as the day he'd said goodbye. But amidst the sorrow, a new feeling began to take root—a realization that Bethany would want him to find happiness again. So many people had told him that over the years, but it always felt like an impossible task.

He set the frame down and sank to his knees beside the couch. With his hands clasped together, he bowed his head. "Lord, I need Your guidance. I don't know what to do. I care for Harper deeply, but I'm afraid. Afraid of forgetting Bethany. Afraid of moving on. Afraid of getting hurt. Please show me the way."

The silence enveloped him, and peace settled over his heart. The turmoil began to ease, replaced by a conviction. Maybe he could honor Bethany's memory by embracing new love. Harper had touched something within him, stirred emotions he hadn't experienced in years.

Rising from his knees, he drew in a new clarity. He had to move forward, not just for himself, but for Emma. Could Harper be the person God placed in his life to help him heal and find joy again?

He touched Bethany's picture again, a silent promise in his heart. "I'll always love you, Bethany. But it's time to live again. For Emma and for me."

With renewed purpose, he turned off the light and headed to bed, his mind awake with thoughts of what the future might hold. As he lay down, a tentative hope bloomed. Tomorrow was a new day, and he prayed he'd be ready to tumble into it with an open heart.

CHAPTER 13

The next morning, with early morning light filtering in through the curtains, Nate dressed and made his way to his mother's house.

When he arrived, Emma ran to him with her usual enthusiasm. "Daddy!"

"Good morning, sweetheart." He scooped her up and hugged her. "Did you sleep well?"

Her eager response bounced her curls. "I had a great sleep. Grandma made pancakes!"

His mother appeared in the doorway, wiping her hands on a dish towel. "Nate, come on in. Breakfast is almost ready. I thought you'd come, so I cooked extra."

Nate set Emma down and followed his mother into the cozy kitchen. The table was already set, the pancakes and syrup scenting the air.

As they ate, she regarded him. "You seem happier this morning. Does it have anything to do with Harper?"

Warmth crept up his neck. "Mom…"

She raised an eyebrow. "Well?"

He huffed. Trying to hide his feelings from her would be useless. "Maybe. I do like her."

"She's a wonderful young woman." His mother beamed. "I think you could be happy together."

He breathed in deeply and released the admission. "I do, too."

"So, what are you going to do about it?"

He forked a piece of pancake and pointed it at her. "I'm not sure yet, but you don't need to make it happen."

She tutted. "I'd never dream of interfering."

He laughed and popped fluffy syrupy goodness into his mouth. "Right."

"Daddy, what are you laughing at?"

He ruffled Emma's hair. "Nothing, sweetheart. Grandma just made a funny comment. That's all."

"Oh, okay."

After breakfast, they bundled up and headed out, walking the short distance to the church. As they approached, excitement tingled through his nerves. While looking forward to seeing Harper, he was also aware of the scrutiny they might face from the close-knit community.

Inside the church, the congregation was already gathering. When she entered with Miriam, his heart gave a little leap, but he stayed with his mother and Emma, not wanting to draw unnecessary attention. As the pair took a seat two rows in front of them, his gaze lingered on Harper.

HARPER STRODE DOWN THE AISLE, still restraining from pirouetting after Nate's hug the previous night. The warmth of his embrace had lingered, countered by the uncertainty of his feelings.

But as much as she wanted to focus on Nate, she had more pressing matters to resolve—her relationship with God.

She settled into her seat next to Miriam, sensing Nate's presence behind her. She glanced back, caught his gaze, and offered a small smile. He returned it, and hope warmed her.

The service began, and she focused on the worship. The songs were uplifting, their words resonating within her. When Pastor Jonathon stepped up to deliver the sermon, she leaned forward, eager to hear his message.

"Today, we're going to talk about the certainty of your faith," he began, his voice steady and reassuring. "How can we be sure of our salvation?"

Harper's heart skipped a beat. This was exactly what she needed to hear.

"Let's read from Ephesians 2 verses 8 and 9," he continued. "'For it is by grace you have been saved, through faith—and this is not from yourselves, it is the gift of God—not by works, so that no one can boast.'" He lifted his gaze. "We need to understand salvation is a gift from God, not something we earn by our own efforts.'"

She'd always felt she needed to prove herself to earn God's love, but she had that wrong. It was by grace alone that she was saved.

"Secondly, we need to trust in the promises of God's Word. The Bible is filled with assurances of His love and commitment to us. Romans 10 verse 9 says, 'If you declare with your mouth, "Jesus is Lord," and believe in your heart that God raised him from the dead, you will be saved.'"

The pastor's words were a balm to her soul. For so long, she'd been trying to figure it out, but here were clear steps to the certainty of salvation.

"Finally, we need to understand that our salvation is secure. In John 10 verses 28 and 29, we read: 'I give them eternal life, and they shall never perish; no one will snatch them out of my hand. My Father, who has given them to me, is greater than all; no one can snatch them out of my Father's hand.'"

Harper's vision blurred. The realization that she was held securely in God's hands, no matter what, was overwhelming. A deep longing to truly embrace her faith washed over her.

As the sermon concluded, Pastor Jonathon invited anyone who wished to renew their commitment to Christ to do so. Harper sucked in a sharp breath. This was her moment. As he asked the congregation to bow their heads, she bowed hers and invited Jesus afresh into her heart.

When the service ended, she slipped an arm around her aunt. "I did it, Aunt Miriam. I invited Jesus into my life, and this time, I meant it."

Aunt Miriam's eyes glistened as she hugged her back. "I'm so happy for you, dear. I've been praying for this moment for years."

AFTER THE SERVICE, Nate, his mother, and Emma entered the bustling church hall. The same hall, filled with warmth during last night's potluck, was again alive with the joyous chatter of those mingling over coffee and tea. As he scanned the room, his gaze found Harper near the refreshment table, speaking with Miriam. Her cheeks were damp, her eyes held a certain glow he hadn't seen before.

Leaving Emma with his mother, he made his way over, his heart beating faster with each step. When he reached her, he touched her arm. "Hey, are you okay?"

She turned to him, her eyes shimmering. "I'm more than okay. The message today—it really touched me. I recommitted my life to the Lord."

His chest swelled. "That's wonderful. I'm so happy for you."

She nodded, her voice trembling. "When I got baptized at summer camp years ago, I didn't understand what a relationship with Jesus meant. I was just following the crowd. But now I know that's what was lacking in my life.

I've been searching for love in all the wrong places, like with Troy, and I've been trying to find my identity in my career. But now I know who I am. A child of God."

Moved by her honesty, he pulled her in for a hug without thinking.

She leaned into him, and the rest of the room faded away. When they stepped apart, he looked into her eyes. "I'm so proud of you, Harper. This is a big step, and I'm here for you."

"Thank you. That means a lot."

He glanced around the room, then took her hand. "I have a day off work tomorrow. I was wondering if you'd like to go skiing."

Her eyes lit. "I'd love that, but I'm very rusty."

"No problem. I can teach you. Let's meet at nine o'clock at the center. Does that work for you?"

She nodded. "Nine it is."

"Wonderful."

CHAPTER 14

*M*orning light cast a warm glow over the room when Harper woke. She stretched and took a deep breath, her mind replaying the previous day—the recommitment to her faith, the warmth of the community, and the invitation to ski.

She dressed in warm layers, choosing a comfortable yet stylish ski outfit Aunt Miriam had insisted she borrow. The soft, insulated fabric hugged her figure, providing the perfect balance of warmth and flexibility. She couldn't help but smile at the prospect of spending the day with Nate.

When she entered the kitchen, Aunt Miriam was already bustling around, preparing breakfast. The smell of freshly brewed coffee and toast tinted the air.

"Good morning, dear," she greeted, her eyes sparkling. "Excited for your skiing adventure today?"

Harper slid into a stool at the island. "I am. But it's

been years since I've skied. I hope I don't embarrass myself."

Aunt Miriam chuckled while placing a plate of scrambled eggs and toast in front of her. "Nate's a great teacher, and you're a quick learner. You'll be fine. Besides, it's about having fun, not perfection."

Harper sipped her coffee, grateful for her aunt's unwavering support. "Thank you, Aunt Miriam. For everything."

As she finished her breakfast, her mind wandered to Nate. His kindness and encouragement touched her deeply. Although she was looking forward to spending the day with him, her stomach fluttered as if mini hopeful ballerinas were trying out for the corps de ballet.

She grabbed her coat, gloves, and scarf and bundled up, getting well-protected against the cold. Aunt Miriam handed her a thermos of hot chocolate. "Something to keep you warm."

"Thank you." Harper gave her a quick hug, then stepped into her boots, and laced them up before heading out the door.

On the invigorating walk to the activity center, naked tree silhouettes and well-dressed pine boughs cast their outlines against the clear sky while crisp air filled her lungs with a sense of freshness and renewal.

A familiar figure walked toward her. "Harper!" Chloe from the quilting group waved. "How nice to see you."

Harper hurried closer. "Nice to see you, too. It's a lovely day, isn't it?"

"Sure is. Would you like to grab a coffee?"

"I'd love to, but I'll need to take a rain check. I'm going skiing today."

Chloe flicked some blonde hair off her round face. "Don't let me stop you, then. Perhaps we can catch up another time."

"I'd like that. Maybe after the quilting session tomorrow?"

"Works for me."

"Perfect. See you tomorrow." Harper continued on her way. Chloe seemed sweet, and although Harper might not be here for much longer, it'd be fun to chat with someone her age.

At the center, Nate was already adjusting the ski equipment. He looked up as she approached, and the warmth of his smile reached deep into her heart. "Good morning. Ready for a day on the snow?"

She breathed in and dug her hands deeper into her pockets. "I think so. It's such a lovely day for it."

"It is. We don't often get days like this. Although there's no guarantee it'll last. The weather can change quickly."

"We'd better make the most of it, then."

"I thought we'd take a Ski-Doo and head to Seven Pines Park." He jerked his thumb to the left where he'd already secured the skis to a two-seater snowmobile similar to the one she'd ridden across the ice bridge with Max. He handed her a helmet, then patted the back seat. "Like to hop on?"

"Sure." After approaching the machine, she swung her leg over the seat and settled in behind him, the warmth of his back comforting in the chilly morning air. Hesitantly, she placed her arms around his waist, feeling the solidness of his frame, the intimacy making her heart race.

He glanced back with a reassuring smile. "Hold on."

She tightened her grip as he started the engine. The snowmobile roared to life, and they took off, the cold wind whipping past. She rested her head against his back, the sensation strangely both thrilling and calming.

On the breathtaking journey to Seven Pines Park, they traveled along snow-covered trails, the landscape a blur of white and green. The pines, firs, and cedars stood majestic, their branches heavy with fresh snow. Meanwhile, icicles dripped off the frigid outlines of dormant maples and oaks, and aspens with their peeling white bark barely stood out against the landscape. They passed an open meadow where the sunlight sparkled on the pristine snow, creating a dazzling display.

He stopped in a clearing and switched off the engine.

She let go of his waist, removed her helmet, and climbed off, her legs wobbly from the ride. She took a deep breath, inhaling the crisp air. "That was amazing."

He grinned as he unstrapped the skis from the snowmobile while she changed into ski boots. "Glad you enjoyed it. Now, let's get you set up for some cross-country skiing." He laid the skis on the ground and handed her a pair of poles.

"I haven't skied in a while, and I've never done cross-country. Is it much different from downhill?"

"It is a bit. Cross-country skiing's more about endurance and rhythm. It's a full-body workout, but it's also really peaceful once you get into the flow of it."

She stepped into the bindings and secured her boots, following Nate's instructions. He adjusted her poles to the right height and then stood back to assess her setup.

"All right, let's start with the basics."

She chuckled as his instructor mode kicked in. But she didn't mind. He looked so handsome, and she could hardly believe they were out here together in this beautiful place.

He stood in front of her. "First, you want to keep your knees slightly bent and your weight centered over your skis. Try to stay relaxed and use your poles to help push forward."

She mimicked his stance, a bit awkward but determined to get it right. She gave him a nod. "I think I've got it."

"Good. Now, we'll start with a simple glide. Push off with one foot and glide forward on the other. Then switch. It's kind of like walking, but with longer strides."

"Similar to ice-skating, just with longer footwear." She winked.

A warm smile brought out hints of his dimple. "Kind of." He demonstrated the motion, gliding over the snow with practiced ease.

She watched, then took a deep breath, and tried to

replicate his movements. Her first few attempts were shaky, but his encouraging smile kept her going.

"That's it. You're doing great." He skied beside her. "Just keep practicing that glide. Remember to use your poles to help with balance and propulsion."

As she continued, she found a rhythm. The initial awkwardness gave way to a smoother motion, and her confidence grew. The crisp air chilled her lungs, and the quiet of the snowy landscape provided a calming backdrop.

"You're getting the hang of it," he praised. "Now, let's try a gentle slope. It'll help you get used to controlling your speed and direction."

They approached a slight decline, and he guided her through the steps. "Keep your weight centered, bend your knees a bit more, and use your poles to control your speed. You've got this."

She took a deep breath and pushed off, gliding down the slope. Her heart raced, but as she reached the bottom smoothly, a rush of accomplishment warmed her.

She bent her knees again, positioning herself as he'd shown her, and stabbed her poles into the ground to follow him. She did well, even getting a few feet in front of him.

Her confidence grew with each glide along the trail. She was enjoying the serene beauty of the snow-covered landscape when her ski caught on a hidden branch and she tumbled forward. One of her skis came off, and the other was at an awkward angle before she landed in a soft pile of snow.

Nate was beside her in an instant. "Are you hurt?"

She looked up, her cheeks flushed, maybe from the cold or the embarrassment. "I don't think so."

He cradled her head, his eyes searching hers. Time seemed to stand still. The world around them faded away, leaving just the two of them. Her heart pounded. Was he about to kiss her? Something unspoken passed between them, a connection both exhilarating and terrifying.

MAN, she was beautiful lying there in his arms, snow surrounding her, cheeks warm and rosy. Nate raised a gloved hand to brush some snow from her face. "As long as you're okay, that's all that matters."

His heart was beating so hard it felt like fists hammering against his ribs as she looked up at him. He moved closer until their foreheads were almost touching. He could so easily kiss her.

But something stopped him.

Pushing away, he unhooked his skis from his boots.

Impulsively, he fisted some snow and squeezed it into a ball. "Harper?"

"Yes?" She sat up and faced him before he tossed the snowball at her chest.

Her eyes widened when he jumped to his feet and

gathered another fistful. Within seconds, he'd launched a second one at her.

"Nate Hawthorn! You're a mischievous man!" She raised her hand defensively, balled up a fistful of snow before scrambling to her feet, and slammed a well-aimed shot at his shoulder.

He scoffed. "Is that the best you've got?"

"Watch and see!" They bent at the same time, forming snowballs in quick succession, hurtling them at each other.

"You won't win this," he said. "I've won the Island Games' Winter Snowball Competition four years running."

"That's only because I wasn't there." She peppered him with snowball after snowball. With her laughter infectious, Nate laughed harder than he had in a long time. She was good. As many snowballs as he fired at her, she matched him.

"How about we call it a draw?" he said when neither were getting the upper hand.

"Giving up, are we?" She raised a brow and tossed another ball.

Breathless, they walked toward each other, laughing with every step. She'd lost her beanie in the fight, and he picked it up where it'd fallen. He dusted away the snow before slipping it onto her head. He removed his glove and brushed a smudge off her cheek, her skin warm beneath his fingers. She looked up at him, her eyes hope-

169

ful, gleaming, and once again, he fought the urge to kiss her.

He pulled back. Was he ready to go down this path? Last night, he'd thought he was, but doubt had crept in again.

He shook his head and forced a grin. "No. We can continue later. We should keep going."

Something—disappointment?—flashed in her eyes. "Okay. That's a deal."

HARPER'S HEART stuttered as Nate grabbed her hands, his laughter rushing around her. Would he kiss her this time?

But the moment ended when he said they should keep going.

He could have kissed her, but he didn't. She didn't get it. When he invited her to go skiing, she got the impression it was a date.

What had she missed?

She let out a heavy breath as he helped her back into her skis. What was holding him back?

Bethany?

Would he ever let her go, or would Harper always be in her shadow if things did progress between them?

She'd just left one relationship where she'd played second fiddle —or third or fourth if she were honest. Troy had never loved her. Not really. She thought he had. Being here on the island had shown her what love was, and it wasn't what she'd had with him. Far from it.

Nate gave her a nod, and they headed off on the snow, her tentatively pushing off with her poles. This time, she stayed upright.

He smiled at her. "You're doing great."

She returned his smile and determined to put her concerns behind her and simply enjoy the day.

They spent the next hour or so skiing through this winter wonderland. By the time they took a break, the sun was high in the sky, casting a golden glow over the snowy landscape. They settled on a log, sipping hot chocolate from the thermos Nate had brought and the one Aunt Miriam had given her.

Head tipped toward the clear sky, she drank in the sunlight. "It's been a lovely day. Thanks for suggesting it."

"You're welcome. I love being outdoors. It helps me think and figure things out." His voice took on a reflective tone. Was he figuring things out now, even as they sat there?

She studied him without making it obvious. "I can understand that. It's so quiet here, so different from the city."

A doe appeared between some trees, looked around, her nose twitching, and then darted back the way she came. Harper smiled. "You don't see that in the city, either."

"I guess not. I've never loved big cities. When Bethany

was ill, we spent months in Detroit while she was having treatment, but we couldn't wait to get back here."

"Tell me about her? I remember seeing her at summer camp, but I didn't know her."

He breathed in slowly and stared into the distance. "Bethany was… amazing. She had this light about her. She always saw the good in people, even when they couldn't see it in themselves. We met on the island. She was visiting her grandparents one summer. I was a bit of a mess back then, trying to figure out my life. When we met, everything just seemed to click."

His eyes softened. Did *he* know the light *he* had around him? How *he* made others see the good in themselves?

"She loved the outdoors as much as I do. We'd spend hours hiking, skiing, or exploring. She was an artist. Painted beautiful landscapes, many of them right here on the island. When she got sick, it was the hardest thing I've ever faced. Watching someone you love suffer, knowing there's little you can do… it's unbearable. But she never complained. She was strong until the end."

He paused as his voice thickened. "What hurts the most is knowing she didn't get to see Emma grow up. She would've been an incredible mother. She did get to hold her, just once. That memory's etched in my mind forever."

Reaching out, Harper covered his hand and squeezed. "She sounds like an amazing woman."

"She was." He turned his hand upward to hold hers, his eyes glistening. "I miss her a lot, but she'd want me to be happy, to find love again."

A moment stretched between them. Harper felt the weight of his grief, but also the hope that had started to take root. Maybe he *could* let go.

"Thanks for sharing that with me." She released his hand. "I can't imagine how hard it's been for you."

He fixed his gaze on her. "I still don't understand why God allowed her to die so young, but the men at my Thursday night group have all suffered loss, and they've helped me understand God must have had something better in mind for her. But it's still not easy."

Harper nodded. "I've still got a lot to learn about God and what it means to trust Him."

He rubbed the back of his neck. "You're not the only one, believe me. It's a lifelong journey, and there's always things to learn. But God's patient and meets us wherever we are along that journey."

Gratitude for God's amazing love swept through Harper. "Just as well, because I messed up badly with Troy."

"We all mess up. The important thing is that you're back on track with God."

"Yes, but it doesn't change the mess I'm in."

"Perhaps not, but He'll lead you through it and help you figure out what to do."

"I hope so because, right now, my career and reputation are in tatters, and my heart's been shattered."

"The guy sounds like a creep. He shouldn't be able to ruin your career just because you don't want to be with him."

A wry chuckle left her lips. "You don't know him. I discovered too late that he's an expert manipulator. He's got the board in his pocket, and he runs the show. He can make careers, and he can ruin them. It's a pity I didn't know that before I fell for him. He's a charmer, and I was searching for love. I was a pushover. Look where it got me."

Compassion peered back at her. "Nothing in life's ever wasted. God can use any experience to grow us if we let Him. You probably learned a lot about yourself, and that's not a bad thing. You can move on from this. You're stronger than you think. God has great things in store for you—I'm sure of it." His soft voice and gentle gaze enveloped her, and his encouragement lifted her.

"Thank you for believing in me. It means a lot."

"You're welcome. Now, we should head back. Otherwise, we might get caught in the storm." He nodded to a dark cloud bank on the horizon.

"Goodness. I hadn't noticed it." She capped Aunt Miriam's thermos. "Good thing you saw it."

He helped her to her feet. "It's my job to keep my clients safe."

Something inside her deflated. Was that all she was? A client?

She studied him again, but when he winked, she knew she'd gotten it wrong.

But what was she to him?

Perhaps he didn't know, either.

The ski back to the snowmobile was uneventful.

Harper kept glancing at the approaching cloud bank, praying they'd get home before the storm hit.

Nate drove her back to Miriam's house as it bordered the nonmotorized area.

She thanked him again for the day, and after a quick hug, he sped away, leaving her more conflicted than ever.

She stomped the snow off her boots on the outside mat, then entered the house, removed her boots, and hung her coat and gloves in the closet before heading toward her room.

"Harper, is that you?" Aunt Miriam called from the kitchen.

Harper paused at the bottom of the staircase. "Yes…"

Her aunt poked her head into the hallway. "Is everything okay? I didn't expect you back so soon."

"Yes, everything's fine." She stiffened her arms at her sides to keep from hugging them around her hollowed-out middle. "We had a lovely day. It looks like a storm's coming, so we headed back a bit early."

"Don't kid a kidder. It doesn't work. Come in here and tell me what's going on."

"Aunt Miriam, I—"

"Come. I'll make you something warm, and we can talk."

Her aunt's tone, though firm, remained gentle. She didn't mean any harm and only wanted to ensure Harper was okay. Except, she wasn't, but she didn't want to admit it. Still, she followed her aunt into the kitchen.

"We do most of our talking in here," Harper noted as

she sat on a stool while Aunt Miriam handed her a bowl of the vegetable soup she'd had heating on the stove.

"The kitchen's the heart of any house. It's the place where we're nourished, in more ways than one. So, tell me how your day was. Truthfully." She pointed the ladle at Harper, then scooped herself a bowl before settling beside her.

Harper stirred the soup, tumbling carrots, peas, and celery over her spoon. "It was lovely. I got the hang of it, as you said I would, and skiing through the Seven Pines Park was amazing. Until I tripped and tumbled." She jabbed at an innocent potato chunk.

"And then what happened?"

Harper shrugged. "I really don't know. Everything was going so well, but then it all changed. Nate changed."

"You've fallen for him, haven't you?"

Harper's shoulders fell. She couldn't deny it. Not to Aunt Miriam. The spoon clattered into the bowl, and she spread her hands. "I've had a crush on him since summer-camp days. I thought I was over him, but spending time with him and Emma confirmed otherwise. But I don't think he feels the same about me."

"And what makes you think that?"

How could she tell her aunt that, when he had the opportunity to kiss her, he didn't take it? She couldn't. "I don't know. It's just a feeling."

Aunt Miriam reached over and clasped her hand. "I think he's as smitten with you as you are with him, but love can take time. There's no need to hurry. If this is God's path for you, it'll happen in His time."

Aunt Miriam might be right, but Harper's time on the island was coming to an end. In fact, now that Aunt Miriam was back, there was no need for her to stay—even though the thought of facing Troy left her cold.

"I need to think about what I'm going to do. Do you mind if I take the soup to my room?"

"Not at all. Let me pray for you first. Is that okay?"

A lump formed in Harper's throat. "That'd be lovely. Thank you."

Aunt Miriam gently clasped Harper's shoulder before closing her eyes. "Heavenly Father, I bring this dear girl before You. Lead and guide her and give her peace about her future, whether that be with Nate and Emma or back in Toronto. Give her clarity about her career and heal her from the hurts of the past. She's been searching for love all her life. May she realize the greatest love of all is found in You. May she grasp how wide and long and high and deep is Christ's love for her. May she know this love that surpasses knowledge—that she might be filled to the measure of all the fullness of Yourself. Bless her now as she ponders these matters, and, Lord, I pray that You'll also be with Nate as he, too, considers his future. In Jesus' precious name, I pray. Amen."

Harper brushed her eyes before she opened them. "Thank you, Aunt Miriam. I appreciate that so much."

"You're welcome, dear. Now, take some time to think and pray, then let me know if you need anything."

Harper slipped off the stool and hugged her. "I will. And thank you again."

Aunt Miriam palmed her cheek. "It's no problem. I just want to see you happy and settled, and like I've said before, you're welcome to stay as long as you want or need."

That was the dilemma. As much as she'd love to stay, her life was in Toronto, not here on this beautiful island. Unless she was given a reason to stay. "I'll pray about it."

"Good girl. Now, let me top up your soup and cut some crusty bread. We don't want you fading away."

Harper chuckled. "Not much chance of that. I've eaten so much since I've been here."

"And you're looking the better for it. You were so thin when you arrived."

"I'm a ballerina."

"Yes, but there's no need to starve yourself."

Harper's chin rose. "I eat enough."

"Really?"

She nodded, although her aunt was right. She didn't eat enough. That was Troy's doing. He was always telling her that, if she wanted to keep her position, she needed to maintain her lithe figure, so she nibbled, not ate. What would he say now if he saw her?

Aunt Miriam placed three thick slices of crusty bread in a small basket and handed it to her. "Take this and enjoy. God bless you, dear." She leaned forward and kissed Harper on the cheek.

"Thank you again." As Harper took the bread and soup

and left the room, the sky darkened, the wind howled, and the icy snow pelted the windows. Nate had made a good call.

In her room, she set her soup bowl and breadbasket on the side table before changing out of her ski gear and slipping on a pair of yoga pants and a warm sweater. She then sat in the wingback chair beside the window, picked up a slice of bread and her bowl of soup, and began eating. The soup was delicious, the bread divine. She'd miss Aunt Miriam's cooking if she left. Oops. That was a Freudian slip. *When* she left.

She released a heavy sigh.

Lord, what am I to do?

If Nate had feelings for her, why wouldn't he say so? If he told her he cared, that might be reason enough to extend her stay. But he'd had the perfect opportunity today, and he hadn't taken it. So all she could assume, despite Aunt Miriam's statement to the contrary, was that he only saw her as a friend.

Besides, if he did want a relationship with her, it would lead to marriage. He wouldn't risk having Emma get hurt.

Was Harper ready for that?

She set her bowl on the side table and closed her eyes. Just as she was about to start praying, her phone rang. She opened her eyes and reached for it. She didn't recognize the number flashing on the screen, but something made her answer it.

"Hello?"

"Harper, it's Amber Richards. Thank goodness I got you. I was beginning to worry I wouldn't reach you in time."

Harper blinked. Amber was one of the other dancers in the company. She'd also been involved with Troy. Whatever prompted her odd call sounded serious. "Why? What's wrong?"

"I know we're not close, but I felt I had to warn you. Troy's auditioning for your position."

Harper's free hand clenched into a ball. It'd been inevitable, but hearing it made it real.

"Harper, are you there?"

"Yes. I'm just taking it in."

"I know it's not the news you wanted to hear. He started auditioning two days ago, and I thought you should know. It's not fair what he did to you. You deserve your spot. You worked hard for it. I know you thought he loved you. I wasn't so blind when I got involved with him. I was taking the easy way to the top, and I thought you were, too—at least until I saw your face when you discovered the truth. If you want to keep your position, you should get back here as soon as possible. I just wanted you to know."

"Thanks. I appreciate you telling me."

"You're welcome."

After the call ended, Harper sat in silence. Troy was doing this. He was going to replace her because she wouldn't return to him.

It was blackmail. She should take him to court. She clenched her fist harder even as her stomach clenched.

Without thinking, she found his number and pressed it. Her body tensed, and she waited for him to answer.

"Harper? Nice to hear from you."

She seethed. "Really?"

"Yes. I've been thinking about you a lot and hoping you'd change your mind."

Her grip on the phone tightened. "You've started auditioning for my position."

"Who told you?"

"It doesn't matter. Is it true?"

"I needed a replacement in case you didn't return. So, are you coming back?"

The million-dollar question.

How did she answer?

She nibbled her lip. "It's over between us. If I come back, will I still have my position?"

"You already know the answer to that."

"I've a fair mind to take you to court."

His tone changed. "But you won't, will you?"

Heat surged through her veins. "You're something else, aren't you?"

"I love you, Harper. The job's still yours if you come back to me. But the clock's ticking."

She slammed the phone down before he could say another word.

She pulled her knees to her chest and rocked as she hugged them, burying her face against them. Then another thought came to her. What if she'd only risen to principal dancer because of her relationship with Troy? What if she wasn't as skilled as she thought?

Her chest hollowed.

Time was against her, and so was Troy. He meant what he said about replacing her. If she wanted to keep her position, she had to return to him.

And she'd never do that.

She could start with a new company, but he'd smear her name out of spite. Her reputation would be in tatters. Could she live with that?

She bowed her head. "Lord, I don't know what to do. My life's such a mess right now. It's hard to think that I might never again dance at that level. That perhaps I only got the position because of Troy. But, Lord, help me to remember my identity as Your beloved child is more important than my career. I'll trust You to show me what You want for me. If that happens to involve Nate, let him tell me he cares for me, because I need to know. In Jesus' name. Amen."

CHAPTER 15

*T*he following morning, with so much on her mind, Harper planned to skip the quilting, but then Grace called to remind her and Aunt Miriam planned to head out. Staying home with her thoughts probably wasn't the best thing, so struggling to muster any enthusiasm, Harper got out of bed, bundled up, and headed across town to Grace's home.

In the town center, the crisp morning air filled her lungs, and the fresh snow glistened on the sidewalks and roads that were yet to be cleared, crunching beneath her boots, creating a rhythmic sound that mirrored her thoughts. The town was waking up, with locals shoveling snow and the occasional passerby offering a friendly nod. Festive lights, still up after the ice-skating evening, twinkled around the gazebo, casting a warm glow over the otherwise gray landscape.

At Grace's home, Harper knocked on the door. It

opened almost immediately, and Grace greeted her with a warm smile.

"Harper! Come in, dear. We've been expecting you."

Stomping off snow on the mat, Harper shrugged off her coat and gloves and handed them to her friend. As she followed her into the cozy dining room, the quilting group's lively chatter drew her in. The women, seated around the large table still laden with colorful fabrics, threads, and quilting tools, turned their heads, their welcoming smiles and cheerful greetings further easing her tension.

She returned their greetings and took her seat beside Chloe.

She needed to be here. The supportive atmosphere and companionship made her feel less alone and helped her almost forget her personal dilemma. But not quite. It hovered in her mind like a grim cloud, leaving her sick inside, the weight pressing heavily.

Over the past weeks, Grace and Nora had taken it upon themselves to teach her to sew, and both had been patient as Harper fumbled along. They sat near her, each working on their piece, but watching over her like mother hens. She liked the feeling.

"Not like that." Grace pointed out. "Like this." She took the piece of fabric Harper was working on and leaned closer. "If you pull the thread this way, it makes the stitch neater."

Harper nodded and tried to get it right. It had taken her some time to decide what story to portray on her quilt patch, but in the end, she'd decided to commemorate her first trip to the island. That trip was the reason she'd had so many after. It was also when she'd met Nate.

Grace peered at the patch belonging to a plump woman seated nearby. "That's looking great, Wendy."

Stilling her fingers, Wendy beamed. "Thanks. I've been working on my sewing skills."

"I can see that." Grace angled her head, adjusting her glasses to study the piece. "Can you tell us about it?"

Wendy's tender gaze dropped to the patch. "It's for my parents. Their choice to move here shaped my life."

Harper and the other women stilled, the emotion in her voice palpable.

"My parents were in their early twenties when they came to Sanctuary Island, not long after the Vietnam War ended. My father was a soldier, and he'd been injured in the war. They came here so he could recover and find peace. He'd seen so much death and pain, and he couldn't settle back in Missouri. He needed a place of refuge, and when a friend told him of the island and the peace he'd found there, it seemed like the perfect place for my father as well."

She pulled her thread through the magenta fabric. "They came that summer. My mother was twenty and had never left her home state. They fell in love with the island and bought a cottage and moved in within weeks of arriving. My mother was expecting me a few months later."

Harper smiled. "That's a lovely story."

Wendy ran her fingers over her patch, tracing the

outline of her design. "Everything I've had in my life was because of that decision. My parents chose to come here, and I was born here. I met my husband here. He sat behind me in grade school and pulled my hair every day. He kept doing it, even when we were teens. When I called him on it, he said he'd been trying to get me to notice him since we were kids."

The room erupted in laughter.

"My husband's a very patient man." Beneath Wendy's nimble fingers, the needle jetéd over the fabric. "I'm grateful to have had the life I've had. My children were raised in a safe place where people care for one another. Now my first grandchild's on the way, and he or she will get a chance to live that life, too. And it's all because of the choice my parents made all those years ago." She lifted her gaze and met Harper's. "You never know the impact your choices will have."

Harper's eyes widened. Did Wendy know she was facing one of the biggest decisions of her life? Surely not.

But her words struck a pose. Harper's decision could have far-reaching consequences and affect more than her. It could affect generations to come. The weight suddenly felt even heavier.

Wendy's story was a happy one. Her parents' decision had worked out for the best.

Harper prayed she, too, would make the right decision.

Although right now, she had no idea what that might be.

Wendy's story ignited a chain of other women telling

their stories. Most had been born on the island, but those who'd moved there as adults all said the same thing—they'd found their piece of paradise.

A pity that Harper's mother hadn't appreciated that paradise. How different her life would have been if she'd stayed. But then, Harper might never have been born. Decisions had consequences.

As the day continued, the food dwindled, and Harper offered to help Grace restock the refreshments. They went into the kitchen to collect more sandwiches and snacks.

Grace stopped her as she was pulling out chips and dip from the cupboard. "Is everything all right, Harper? You seem distracted."

Did she? Hadn't she managed to put on a bright face? She waved off the comment. "I'm still thinking things through. That's all."

"If you want to talk, I'm always happy to be a sounding board."

"And I appreciate that." Harper gave a warm smile. "It's complicated. That's all."

Grace patted her back. "I'll pray for you. God will help you figure it out."

They'd almost finished replenishing the platters when Nate entered the kitchen. Harper's heart jolted. What was he doing here?

As he kissed his mother on the cheek, his gaze caught Harper's, and he stilled. "I didn't know you were here."

She shifted and busied herself with the platter, lining

the crackers up like dancers at a barre. "It's quilting morning."

"I forgot. How's it coming along?"

She nodded, still not meeting his gaze. "Quite well. Grace and Nora have been patient with me."

Grace linked her arm through Harper's and tugged her over. "She's a quick learner. You should see her work. We were just getting some snacks together. Would you like something?"

He gripped the back of a chair. "I'm okay for now. I just dropped by to say hello. I'd forgotten all about the quilting session."

"You're welcome to stay."

He hooted a low laugh. "Thanks, but I'll leave you to it."

His gaze was still on her. An unresolved tension lingered between them, and she could see it in his eyes, feel it in the air.

It must have been obvious because Grace eyed them, then said she'd take the platter to the ladies. When she was gone, neither spoke.

Finally, he broke the silence. "I enjoyed yesterday."

She forced herself to face him. "Same here. It was fun."

"We should do it again sometime."

She felt like her heart was being torn from her chest. "I might not be here much longer."

"Oh? What's happened?" His voice was soft now.

"One of the other dancers called me last night. Troy's auditioning for my position."

"I'm so sorry." Nate stepped around the table and placed his hands on her upper arms.

She leaned into the touch, willing him to say more. To give her a reason to stay. Her throat clogged as she pushed down the sobs forming in her chest.

"Don't let him replace you without a fight unless it's what you want."

Her chest hollowed. "If only it were that simple."

"It can be. You just need to decide what you want to fight for."

"That's the problem." Gazing into his brown eyes, she knew she loved him. But did she love him enough to give up her career, especially when he was still in love with Bethany?

"Perhaps things will become clear if you go back."

Her heart clenched at the thought of leaving the island. And him.

She exhaled, but the breath rushed from her lungs like hope hissing free, escaping, evaporating. "Perhaps you're right."

"Emma will miss you if you go."

And would he? Why wouldn't he say something?

"I'll miss her, too. She's such a special girl. I need to think about it, but I can't stay here forever. My life's in Toronto. Everything I have is there."

His gaze lingered on her. "Then you need to get back to that life. Don't worry about Troy and what he's trying to pull. Figure out what you want and go for it. God has wonderful things in store for you, and if they're in

189

Toronto, then they'll come to you regardless of what Troy tries to do."

True. She needed to face Troy, if nothing else. She couldn't let him get away with his bullying tactics. She needed to expose his unethical behavior and prevent him from treating other dancers in the way he'd treated her and Amber.

Grace reentered the room and headed straight to the kettle. "Sorry to interrupt. I need to refill the teapot."

"It's okay." Harper sniffed. "Nate's been helping me figure out what I need to do."

Grace stopped and looked between them again, her eyes pinprick sharp. "And dare I ask?"

Nate searched Harper's eyes. "Do you want to tell her what's happened?"

She sucked in a breath. "I probably should." She shifted her gaze to Grace. "My boss is auditioning for dancers to replace me."

"Oh, my dear girl. Why would he do that?"

Nate replied for her. "Because he's a bully."

Grace crossed the floor and hugged her. "Is that why you came to the island? Because you were being bullied?"

Harper nodded into her shoulder. "Something like that."

"Oh, you sweet girl. I hate seeing people I care about being bullied. I hate bullying altogether. You should have told me. I'd have helped you."

"It's okay. It was something I had to figure out for myself."

"You don't have to accept that kind of mistreatment. There are other dance companies, and with your credentials, you won't have any trouble finding another position. You always have choices." Grace raised her brow at Nate before turning back to Harper. "And you could always stay here on the island. I know a little girl who'd be ecstatic if you did."

Nate glared at his mother. "Don't manipulate. Harper needs to decide for herself."

Grace patted his arm. "I'm not. I'm simply stating the truth. I'll fill the teapot and leave you to talk. Come back in when you're ready, dear."

The idea of returning to the room with a bunch of ladies, as nice as they were, didn't thrill her. "I'll just head home if you don't mind. I need time to think."

"No problem. I'll pack up your sewing and let the ladies know you had to leave. They'll understand."

"Thank you. Oh, and can you tell Chloe we'll need to catch up another time?"

"Sure."

When she left, Nate rubbed the back of his neck. "Would you like me to walk with you?"

"Thanks, but I need to be alone for a bit."

"I'll call you later."

"I'll look forward to it." With her chest clogging, she fled down the hall, grabbed her coat, and left the house, her tears just below the surface. Nate didn't care for her. He'd told her to go back to Toronto. If he had feelings for her, he would have asked her to stay. How had she gotten it so wrong?

When Harper returned, her aunt called out to her. Harper had been heading straight for her room, but stopped, and poked her head in the studio doorway.

Aunt Miriam stood at an easel and waved her in. "Take a look at this."

Harper took a steadying breath, wiped her face, and stepped into Miriam's art studio, a small room off the living room with skylights in the sloping ceiling and large windows letting in natural light. Art paraphernalia cluttered every corner, and potted plants, paint cans, brushes, and spatulas covered the brightly colored shelves and dressers. Paint splatters marked the floor, years of work layered on top of each other, and the smell of acrylic paint lingered in the air. A confusing mix of colors blotched Aunt Miriam's painting.

"It looks like chaos."

Her aunt laughed. "It only looks like chaos because you don't have the right perspective. Once you see it clearly, then you'll also see the hidden beauty."

Harper forced a smile. "That's quite deep."

Aunt Miriam removed her glasses and peered at her. "Is everything okay?"

Harper let out a heavy sigh. "I'm just tired. If you don't mind, I'll take a nap. Don't worry about lunch for me. I'll fix myself a sandwich when I'm ready."

Aunt Miriam fiddled with her glasses. "Are you sure?"

"Yes." Harper kissed her aunt's cheek and headed to

her room. After closing the door, she climbed onto the bed and hugged a pillow as her aunt's words played in her head.

"It only looks like chaos because you don't have the right perspective."

She closed her eyes. "Lord, help me to have the right perspective so I can see my way through this chaos."

CHAPTER 16

*L*ava-hot heat swept through Nate. Who did Troy think he was? He couldn't have Harper, so he was trying to replace her? Did he think it was that simple? That no one would care?

Well, the dude was wrong.

He leaned into the cold, his hands deep in his pockets, and strode to the parking lot. He hopped onto his Ski-Doo and took off cross-country toward Elijah's garage, the wind whipping his face. If anyone could help him think clearly, his best friend could.

He turned into the garage driveway at speed, sending a spray of snow into the air as he banked right and brought the Ski-Doo to a stop outside the snowmobile bay.

Elijah rushed out, his eyes wide. "Nate? What's going on?"

Nate got off his machine. "A lot. Can we talk?"

Elijah nodded, wiping his hands on a rag. "Sure. Come

inside." He placed an arm across Nate's shoulders and walked him inside.

Nate flopped onto the couch, his elbows on his knees, and clasped his hands.

"What's happened?" Elijah closed the door.

Nate filled his lungs. "Harper might leave." Not the words he'd planned to say, but the first to leave his lips. He stood and began pacing, raking his fingers through his hair.

"Slow down. What're you talking about?"

Nate stopped pacing and faced his friend. "There's this guy who's trying to force her to do something she doesn't want to. If she doesn't stand up to him, he's going to replace her, and she won't have a job."

"Are you serious? There are people out there who do that kind of thing?"

"Yeah. Seems this jerk has the power to destroy her career and he wants to." Nate gritted his teeth. "I told her she needs to stand up to him."

"And that means her leaving." Elijah leaned against his desk and folded his arms. "But you don't want her to, right?"

Nate huffed out a breath. Of course he didn't want her to leave. Why was it so hard to admit that to his friend?

And to her?

The sudden burst of energy alleviated some of his anger, and he flopped onto the couch once again. "She came here to figure things out. I'm afraid this guy's threats will cause her to make the wrong choice."

"And what choice is that?"

"To leave."

Elijah held up both palms. "And why should that bother you?"

Nate frowned. "What do you mean?"

"As far as I know, you and Harper are just friends. She lives in Ontario. If she goes back, it shouldn't mean anything to you. You're 'just friends,' or so you've told me."

Nate averted his gaze. "Don't start that."

"Start what? I'm standing here listening to the fears of a man who says he doesn't have feelings for a woman when he clearly does. I'm not the one in denial."

Nate swung his gaze back to his friend, words of rebuttal on his tongue, but as he attempted to utter them, he couldn't.

Who was he kidding? Harper wasn't just a friend.

He hung his head in his hands. "This is so confusing."

Elijah crossed the room and dropped onto the couch beside him. "No, it's not. There's nothing confusing about falling in love, except when it's you. You've been denying yourself the chance for so long that you don't know what to do."

Nate rubbed his eyes. The sting behind them couldn't be tears. "You don't know how this feels."

"So, tell me."

Nate leaned back against the couch and took a deep breath. "I can't help it. I think about her every day. Several times a day."

He released the breath, his chest deflating. "I haven't felt this way in years. Not since Bethany. At first, I didn't want to admit it because it felt as if I was betraying her, but I can't pretend I don't have feelings for Harper." He swallowed hard and lifted his gaze. "Because I do. I knew she was only here for a short time. I shouldn't have gotten close, but I let her into my life, into my mother's life, and into Emma's life. I didn't try to stop it, even though I knew I should. Harper was always going to leave, but I kept getting close. Kept wanting to be with her. Now, she might leave, and where will that leave us?"

"Have you told her how you feel?"

He palmed the back of his head, kneading tense muscles. "No. How can I? She didn't come here to fall in love. She came to get her life in order. How would it be fair if I dumped my feelings on her, expecting her to give up everything to be with me?"

"But that would be her choice, wouldn't it? If you don't tell her how you feel and she makes the wrong choice because she didn't know, whose fault is that?" Elijah slapped Nate's knee. "If you have feelings... and let's not beat around the bush, you love the girl. If you love her but don't tell her she has a choice to stay with you and to be loved by you, you'll have robbed you both of the opportunity of a future together."

Nate pressed harder at the knots on his neck. "The truth is, I'm scared."

Compassion peered back at him. "I understand."

Nate pushed to his feet and paced to the window, but

the view blurred as he blinked back tears. "I did every-thing for Bethany. I loved her with all that I had, and I lost her. First Dad, then her."

"You weren't responsible for their deaths. Your father's was an accident, and Bethany's was out of your control."

Nate gripped the windowsill, his muscles taut. "But I should have been there. I was supposed to take the tour, not Dad. He tried to save that kayaker and drowned because I was elsewhere."

"But you were there for Bethany. You did everything you could for her, but you're not God. You can't take responsibility for life and death. We don't see things the way God does, and we might never understand why He allows things like that to happen—but we can be sure He still loves us and has our back."

Tears rolled down Nate's cheeks. "It hurt so much to lose them." He released the windowsill and shifted to lean back against it. "I've done everything in my power to make sure Emma stays safe so I won't lose her. I haven't dated anyone because I didn't want to bring someone into our lives who might leave. I wanted to protect her. And me."

"And how's that worked for you? Are you any happier?"

He scrubbed his face with his hands. "No."

"You can't protect yourself by putting up barriers. When you do that, you prevent the good as well as the bad, and if I can be honest with you, it was never going to last. I've known you my entire life, and I know how big your heart is. One day, someone was bound to come along, get past your excuses, and make you happy. I think Harper's that person. You saw how easily she got into your heart. How easily she found a place in your family. It's almost as if she was sent by God."

"Elijah—"

"Hear me out." Elijah held up a hand. "Even if you tell her how you feel, there's no guarantee she'll stay. But if you don't tell her and she leaves, not telling her will haunt you for the rest of your life. You'll always wonder what might have been, but you'll never know. You've got a second chance at love. Take it. There's nothing wrong with it. Yes, Bethany's still in your heart, and no one can replace her. She was your wife, she's Emma's mother, and you loved her for a long time. But that can't stop you from being able to love."

Nate raked his hands through his hair. "I don't know."

"Yes, you do. You want to tell her. You wouldn't be here if you didn't want to. Somewhere inside, you wanted me to tell you it was okay to love her. But you don't need my permission." Elijah locked his hands together and held them up as if praying or pleading. "I've been praying for this day for years. You just need to take the first step. Leave the outcome with God. But He won't force you to do anything, so the next step is yours."

"But what if telling her makes things harder for her?"

"It's already hard. I doubt telling her would make it worse. If anything, it might be the best thing for you both." Elijah lowered his hands and gripped his knees.

"Have you ever considered how she feels about you? She might be waiting for you to make a move and tell her how *you* feel."

"You might be right." He'd often sensed she was holding something back but hadn't allowed himself to dig beneath the surface.

"The question is…" Elijah rose and crossed to his side. "What are you going to do about it?"

"Pray."

"Good man." Elijah's shoulder jostled his. "I'll pray for you, too."

"Thanks."

Elijah gave him a bear hug. "God be with you, man."

"And with you."

Elijah walked with him back to his Ski-Doo. Nate climbed aboard, less tense than when he arrived. He put on his helmet and nodded to Elijah before riding to the parking lot.

After parking, he walked briskly to the school, which wasn't far past his mother's home. As he approached the school, Tom Fuller was standing by the entrance, chatting with another parent. The fifth- and sixth-grade teacher was also a widower and attended the Thursday night support group.

"Hey, Tom!" Nate called out after he'd ended the conversation with the other parent.

Tom waved. "Nate! How's it going?"

Nate shrugged. "Busy as always. Just here to pick up Emma. How are things with you?"

"Good, good. Just finished up for the day. I haven't seen you at the group lately. Is everything okay?"

How did Nate answer that? He ran a hand around his neck. "Yeah. I've met someone."

"Really?" Tom clicked his fingers. "The ballerina! I saw you together at the ice-skating night and then again at the potluck. So, how's it going?"

Nate's gut twisted. "It's complicated."

Tom clapped him on the back. "In our situation, it's always going to be complicated. But if this is what God wants for you, He'll help you figure it out. I'll be sure to pray for you."

"Thanks, man. I appreciate it. I'll try to make it to the next meeting."

"Good. I'll look forward to seeing you there."

Emma ran up, her face beaming. "Daddy, can we go to the park?"

He swung her into his arms and hugged her. "Maybe. But I thought we might go sledding."

"Sledding! Yay! Let's go."

He grinned at Tom and strolled off with Emma.

After a quick snack, they bundled up. Minutes later, she chattered nonstop as they pulled out the old toboggan from the shed. After yesterday's storm, the snow was perfect for sledding—the fun way to spend the afternoon would also get his mind off Harper for a while.

They made their way to the hill behind the house, Emma chattering about her day at school. Nate listened with one ear, his thoughts drifting back to Harper. He couldn't shake his conversation with Elijah. His friend's words echoed in his mind, mingling with his own fears and hopes.

"Ready, Daddy?" Emma's voice snapped him back to the present. She was already seated on the toboggan, beaming up at him.

"Ready." He gave her a push and then ran alongside as she zoomed down the hill. Her laughter filled the air, the joyful sound warming his heart, even in the cold.

As they trudged back up the hill for another go, Emma's excitement bubbled over. Halfway up, she stopped and, with a twirl of determination, attempted a ballet pirouette just as Harper had shown her. She spun around once before losing her balance and tumbling into the snow, giggling.

Nate laughed, helped her up, and brushed the snow from her coat. "You're getting better at that, sweetheart."

She beamed, her eyes sparkling. "Harper taught me how to do it. She said that if I try hard and practice, I might dance as well as she does. She has such pretty hair. It's not long like mine, but she looks good with it. And the other day, when we were with Grandma, she helped me make my sandwich. I like having her as my friend. I don't want her to leave, but Grandma says she might. Will she still be my friend even if she does? I hope so. She makes me feel good. She talks to me differently than other grown-ups. She doesn't just tell me what to do, but we play, and she teaches me things like you and Grandma do. She's what I think Mommy would be like."

Nate blinked as her word barrage reached deep inside.

And crushed any denial he had about Harper's impact on his daughter. He'd have to be deaf not to hear the loving admiration in Emma's voice. Harper had a place in both their hearts, a place he couldn't ignore.

Not anymore.

"Don't worry about if Harper will go back home," he said. "Just enjoy the time with her now. Who knows what might happen?"

"Only God does." His daughter's dimples peeked out.

"You got that from Grandma, huh?"

She nodded with a toothy grin. "Yes."

"Come on. Let's have some more rides before we go in." Nate held her hand up the rest of the hill.

They spent the next half hour sledding, Emma's giggles and squeals grounding him in the moment. But as they headed back inside, cheeks rosy and noses cold, thoughts of Harper returned with full force.

If he told her how he felt, would she reject him? Would his confession send her fleeing?

She cared about Emma, but did she want a child in her life?

Did thinking of this even make sense when he hadn't yet told her how he felt?

A lot of things were up in the air, but she still had a choice to make. Troubling her with his feelings when she had a life-altering decision to make seemed selfish.

But if he didn't tell her how he felt, would he regret it like Elijah said he would?

Yes.

If she had feelings for him but still wanted her career, could he pack up and move Emma to Ontario? How would his mother cope? She and Emma were so close.

Could he tear them apart?

There seemed to be no answer, and the more he asked, the more questions popped up.

Let her choose.

The words rose in his spirit while he prepared dinner. He couldn't deny his feelings any longer. Elijah was right. Nate needed to tell her how he felt, to give her the option to stay. He prayed silently, asking God for the courage to be honest with her and for guidance on how to move forward.

Later, he read a story to Emma like he always did. After she said her prayers, he stayed with her, watching her slow, even breaths as sleep overtook her. Tucked under her arm was a ballerina doll, a present from Harper a few days earlier. He leaned over and kissed her forehead before tucking her in and leaving the room.

She already loves Harper. The thought came to him when he pulled the door closed behind him. Harper cared about her, too. If he told her how he felt, maybe they could be a family.

He walked to the living room, sat in his armchair in front of the fire, and opened his Bible, flipping through the familiar pages, searching for comfort and clarity. The words of Proverbs 3:5–6 stood out:

Trust in the LORD with all your heart and lean not on

your own understanding; in all your ways submit to him, and he will make your paths straight.

He took a deep breath, letting the words sink in. He needed to trust God with this, to submit his fears and hopes to Him. He closed his eyes and bowed his head. "Lord God, give me the strength to be honest with Harper and help me to trust You with the outcome. You know how I feel about her, but Your will be done, not mine."

CHAPTER 17

*H*ow did one change their perspective? Harper had thought by morning she'd be clear on what to do, but she wasn't. Instead, she was focused on how she was seeing her situation. Like Miriam's painting, her life was chaos. Yet, through the chaos, Miriam was sure something beautiful would emerge. Even standing beneath a hot shower, the water cascading over her head, Harper remained unsettled. All she wanted was clarity, but nothing seemed to bring it.

The joy of the Lord is your strength. The words reverberated in her mind. She'd read them recently in one of Miriam's Bibles. She didn't understand why people had more than one version of the Bible until she got to know Miriam better. Her great-aunt had three versions, and having glanced through them in comparison, Harper now understood why. Some made things simpler to understand, while others used older language that she couldn't make heads or tails of, but the essence was the same. She found comfort in that. The Word of God. It was something she never thought possible.

She returned to her room. She should pack but couldn't bring herself to start. She'd take a walk instead.

It could be her last before she left.

Aunt Miriam looked up as Harper headed for the door, her spectacles on the edge of her nose, a breath away from falling off. "Going out?"

Harper paused. "Just need to stretch my legs."

Her aunt smiled. "Okay. Don't go too far. According to the forecast, we might be in for a bit more weather, although I never rely on what they say. They get it right half of the time at best."

Harper stepped outside and adjusted her scarf to ward off the cold creeping down her neck. Despite the forecast, the sky was a lovely cornflower blue, sparsely dotted with clouds, and the weak winter sun shone on pristine snow. Maybe things would stay mild, but some thicker clouds in the distance cast doubt.

She went on, inhaling the crisp air deep into her lungs and expelling it in a plume of white cloud as she walked along the sidewalk, the faint sound of children laughing and a bird chirping in a nearby tree the only sounds.

When she reached the boardwalk, an older woman she recognized from the quilting group approached. "Hello, Mrs. Waterman."

The woman was bundled up tightly, her nose and eyes

all that could be seen beneath her layers of clothing, but her florescent-orange jacket disclosed her identity.

She raised a hand in return, her words muffled beneath the scarf wrapped around her face. "Good morning, Harper. Bundle up if you plan to be out for a while. The weather report said things may turn bleak."

She smiled at the woman. "I'll be sure to do that. You do the same."

Never had Harper had so many people who cared about her well-being the way the people on the island did. It would be so hard to leave and return to the city.

Her footsteps echoed hollow along the boardwalk heading toward the lighthouse. With the wind picking up, she pulled her jacket tighter. Reaching the lighthouse, she stood overlooking the frozen lake toward the mainland.

She'd been on the island for over a month now. So much had changed. With the Lord now in her life, she could face whatever lay ahead, but what did He want her to do? Go back and fight for her position? Strange, but that life no longer appealed. It was exciting, glitzy, and glamorous, and she loved to dance—no denying that. But she wanted more.

She wanted a family.

Those few days when she thought she might have been carrying a child had changed her perspective. She'd never considered being a mother until then, but when she discovered she wasn't expecting, the loss had been real.

Aunt Miriam promised she could stay as long as she wanted. "Lord, is that what You want me to do? Stay here?

Even if Nate only sees me as a friend? I should be able to deal with that. Plenty of people do, but I've loved him for so long...." She breathed in deeply and pushed back tears. "Now, I don't know I could handle seeing him every day if we weren't together. It'd be easier if I never saw him again."

An engine's whir broke through the howling wind.

She looked along the path, and warmth surged through her. Nate was riding toward her.

After pulling the Ski-Doo to a stop, he got off and strode to her.

She met his steady gaze. "How did you find me?"

"Mrs. Waterman told me you were headed this way." He stepped closer. "I need to tell you something."

The earnestness in his eyes made her heart thrum. "Yes?"

"I know I told you yesterday that you should go back and face Troy, but the truth is, I don't want you to leave."

Her throat closed.

"Over the past weeks as I've gotten to know you, I've struggled with the thought of letting go of Bethany. But I've come to understand that, while I'll always love her, there's room in my heart for another. I don't know how you feel about me. I *do* know I'm falling for you and I'd love it if you chose to stay on the island and see where this might take us. I don't know how that would affect your career, but—"

She held up her hand. "I don't care about my career anymore. I've been praying for clarity, and I have it. I love dancing, and for a while, it fulfilled me, but now I want more than that. The love and acceptance I've felt here on the island have shown me how shallow that life was. I want to live somewhere where I belong. With people I truly care for. With people I love."

She swallowed hard as she held his gaze. "I love you, Nate. I've loved you for a long time. Ever since summer camp. Back then, it was a teenage crush, but now, it's proper love. You're an amazing man, a wonderful father, and I want to stay and see where this will take us."

He gathered her into his arms and held her snugly. "I'm so glad to hear that."

She leaned into him, his warmth reaching her through their jackets.

When snowflakes tumbled around them, he drew her even closer, brushed his lips against her forehead, and then tipped her chin upward, gazing into her eyes for a heartbeat before bending down to capture her lips. His kiss was slow and tender, and her hands slipped around his neck, pulling him closer as she melted into his embrace.

His arms were strong, his chest solid, his touch confident, conveying how much he cared for her in a language far more expressive than words. It was everything a first kiss should be, and it ended far too soon. Even after breaking the kiss, he kept his arms around her, holding her close against him, his breathing as uneven as hers. "I'd say we've officially moved beyond friendship." His moist breath murmured over her.

"So, what do we do now?"

"We could stay here and freeze, or I could give you a ride home."

She scooted back to examine his face. "I didn't mean that."

He cupped her cheek and grinned. "I know. The answer is, I'm not sure. But let's start by having dinner tonight."

"That sounds wonderful. Would you like me to cook?"

His brow quirked. "You don't trust my cooking?"

"I didn't say that."

"No, you didn't. Thanks for the offer, but Emma and I will cook. She'll be excited."

"Okay. Let me bring some dessert."

"Deal. Now, let's get out of here." He grabbed her hand, and together they sprinted to the snowmobile.

She jumped on the back.

He handed her a helmet, then climbed on the front, and fired it up. "Hold on."

She slipped her arms around his waist. In that moment, an indescribable warmth—*love*—surrounded her. She gazed across the lake as they sped back toward town. "Thank You, Lord, for giving me clarity at last."

He dropped her off at Miriam's and promised to pick her up at five. "I don't want you walking, especially if it storms." He pulled her in for another kiss before driving away.

She could barely believe the events since leaving the house just two hours before. She breathed in deeply, savoring the sensation of being truly happy and blessed. And loved.

She clomped the snow off her boots, entered the house, and put away her coat and boots, calling out in the stillness. "Aunt Miriam?"

"In the studio."

Harper headed there. Her aunt was sitting at her potter's wheel, elbow-deep in clay.

Harper laughed as she stepped closer. "What's this?"

"Another project I'm working on for the Annual Extravaganza. It came to me last night, so I decided to start it today."

"Do you always do the things that pop into your mind?"

"When you get to be my age, you don't have time to dawdle." Her aunt focused on the piece as it spun on the wheel. She dampened a sponge and put it against the side of the sculpture to help shape it. "How was your walk?"

Harper couldn't help but grin. "Good."

Her aunt stopped the wheel and studied her. "I'm guessing he found you?"

"You mean Nate?"

She nodded.

"How did you know he was looking for me?"

"He came here. I told him you'd gone for a walk."

"Oh." A warm glow radiated inside her. "Yes, he found me at the lighthouse."

"And can I be a nosy old aunt and ask what happened?"

Harper's legs twitched. Before she could stop herself,

she performed a little spin and a petit saut. "He told me he doesn't want me to leave."

"So, you're staying?"

Harper bowed with a flourish. "If the invitation's still open."

"Of course, it is! I love having you around. And so does Sir Greyson."

On cue, the cat strolled into the room and wove around Harper's legs. She picked him up and snuggled him. "You still remember me, do you?" Since Aunt Miriam had returned, he'd barely given Harper a meow, but he meowed now.

She shook her head and held him until he wriggled and she set him down. "Nate's invited me to dinner. I said I'd take dessert, so I'd better figure out what to make."

"Apple pie's always a winner. I've got all the ingredients, so you won't need to trek to the store."

"Wonderful. I'll make a start."

She headed to the kitchen and gathered the ingredients, setting them on the kitchen counter. She mixed the sugar, cinnamon, and nutmeg with the canned apples, the aroma sweetening the kitchen. As she rolled out the dough, she caught herself humming, thinking about the unexpected turn her life had taken.

After carefully placing the apple mixture into the piecrust, she covered it with another layer of dough and crimped the edges before brushing the top with an egg wash and sprinkling it with sugar.

Then she slid the pie into the oven and set the timer.

She still had half a day to fill before Nate picked her up. She'd planned to pack, but now there was no need, so she'd read and work on her quilting patch. Grace had told her the quilt was going to be displayed at the Extravaganza in a few weeks' time. Harper hadn't expected to be on the island then, but now? She very well could be.

As she settled into a chair with her book, she tried to focus, but her mind kept wandering to the future and what tomorrow and the tomorrows after that might look like. Who could believe she, Nate, and Emma might one day be a family? But she was tumbling ahead. He hadn't told her he loved her, just that he had room in his heart for another and he was falling for her. It was almost enough to believe it might blossom into love.

WHEN NATE PULLED up outside Miriam's house, dark clouds hovered overhead, and light snowflakes twirled and danced on the breeze. He climbed off his Ski-Doo and hurried along the walkway to the front door.

Just as he was about to knock, Harper opened it and greeted him with a smile. "Hey."

"Hey, yourself. You look gorgeous."

A pretty blush pinked her cheeks. She lowered her gaze. "Thank you."

"You're welcome. Are you ready?"

She held up a hand. "Let me grab my coat and the

dessert. But come in out of the cold. I'll only be a moment."

He stepped inside the entry as she hurried down the hallway, returning moments later with an insulated carry case.

"Apple pie?"

She beamed. "Yes."

"It smells amazing."

She chuckled. "I hope it tastes as good as it smells. I used Aunt Miriam's recipe."

"I'm sure it will."

She wiggled into her boots and grabbed her coat. Then he helped her with it, pausing to take in everything about her. Harper Mackenzie short-circuited his lungs. The slender arch of her neck, the warmth to her eyes, and the gentle curve of her jaw… lovely.

He held her hand as they walked to his Ski-Doo. She climbed on behind him and placed the carry case between them before slipping one arm around his waist.

He took the shortest route down to the lake and alongside Harbor Way to the parking lot. Despite him wearing a helmet and tucking his scarf around his neck and chin, icy wind penetrated the gaps and nipped at his skin.

They reached the parking lot and dismounted.

Harper was shivering.

He draped his arm around her shoulders. "It's freezing, isn't it?"

She nodded, her teeth chattering.

"Let me carry that." He reached for the carry case. When she handed it over, he tucked it under his free arm. "It's not far, but we'll need to walk fast so we don't turn into icicles."

"I'm glad you picked me up. I wouldn't have liked to walk the entire distance tonight. I've not known it to be so cold in the time I've been here." Her breath created small clouds in the cold air.

"Windchill's high tonight with the wind coming straight off the lake."

"I guess I'll have to get used to it now that I'm staying."

And those four words chased the chill away.

At his house, he opened the door, and warmth enveloped them. Emma's laughter echoed from the living room, and his mother appeared in the hallway, her eyes lighting when she sighted Harper.

"So good to see you, dear." Mom hugged Harper before stepping back. "Dinner's ready, and Emma's in the living room coloring. Let me know when you'd like me back."

"You're not staying?" Harper's brow furrowed.

"I need to work on the quilt. And I'm sure you don't want me on your first date." Mom winked and stepped into her boots.

He placed the container on the hall table, helped her into her coat, then kissed her cheek before she opened the door.

"Thanks, Mom. Hope you don't freeze. Are you sure you don't want me to walk you home?"

She gave a backward wave. "I'll be fine. It's only two blocks."

"Okay, then." He closed the door and rested a hand on the small of Harper's back. "Welcome to my humble abode."

She rose onto tiptoes, craning around, her eyes wide. "It's lovely."

Her warmth seeped into his palm through her thin cashmere sweater. "You're too kind. I'm refurbishing, but it's taking ages. This entry really needs some TLC."

"I don't know what you mean." Her impish grin made him laugh.

When she went to remove her coat, he stepped forward and helped her, but he paused as their gazes met. He cupped her cheek and lowered his mouth. She wrapped her arm around his neck, and he deepened the kiss.

A giggle, like the tinkling of bells, broke the moment. He stepped back, and Harper did the same.

Emma stood there, grinning.

Nate smiled at his daughter. "Hey, sweetie."

"What are you and Harper doing?"

Harper's cheeks flared red. "Um, we were…"

"Kissing." Emma giggled. "Does that mean Harper's going to be my new mommy?"

Nate shrugged before he crouched down to Emma's height. "We'll have to wait and see. Now, let's show Harper to the kitchen, shall we?"

AN EMOTIONAL WHIRLWIND swept through Harper as Emma took her hand and led her down the hallway. The warmth of Nate's home enveloped her, and the rich, comforting scent of home cooking beckoned her into the kitchen. With Emma's excitement contagious, Harper smiled, despite the lingering blush from their kiss.

"This is our kitchen!" Emma let go of Harper's hand to run ahead, sliding in her socked feet across the hardwood floor.

Cozy and inviting, the space offered warm oak cabinets and dark granite counters cluttered with mini appliances. A mix of vintage and modern elements created a charming, eclectic vibe, and a vase of fresh flowers basked in the evening sun on the windowsill. Magnets held family photos to the fridge, including several of him and Bethany. What a stark contrast to her sleek, minimalist apartment in Toronto. Nate's home felt lived-in and loved. It didn't need refurbishment.

Harper's heart swelled at Emma's enthusiasm. The little girl's joy reminded her of simpler times.

Nate followed, carrying the insulated case with the apple pie. "Make yourself at home." He placed the carry case on the counter. "Dinner will be ready in a few minutes."

She nodded, feeling a bit like an intruder in this intimate setting while taking in the details. He'd clearly put thought into every aspect of his home.

A small chalkboard on the wall displayed a hand-written menu for the evening: spaghetti Bolognese, garlic bread, and salad. Simple, yet comforting. A far cry from the gourmet meals she was used to in Toronto, but perfect for the occasion.

"Can I help with anything?" She stepped closer to him.

He shook his head, his eyes warm. "Just relax. You're our guest tonight."

Emma tugged at her sleeve. "Come see my coloring!"

Harper followed her to the living room where coloring books and crayons covered a large wooden coffee table with child-friendly rounded edges. Equally as cozy as the kitchen, the room invited one to relax on the soft, worn-in couch while a fireplace added to the homey atmosphere. More family photos lined the mantel, and a stack of brightly colored, little books beckoned from a side table.

As Emma displayed the latest masterpiece, Harper savored a sense of belonging she hadn't experienced in a long time. This felt right, being here with Nate and Emma, sharing a meal, and enjoying each other's company.

Nate called them to the kitchen as the spaghetti was ready. They gathered around the table, Emma chattering about her school day and the fun they had sledding yesterday. Harper couldn't stop smiling, her heart full of warmth and affection for this little family.

Nate extended his hands. "Shall we give thanks?"

Harper reached out and took his hand in one of hers

and Emma's in the other. His hand was warm and strong, Emma's soft and vulnerable. Holding his evoked a promise of dependability while holding Emma's carried a fearsome responsibility. Yet peace soothed her as they bowed their heads.

"Lord, thank You for this food and for bringing us together tonight." Nate offered the simple grace. "Bless this meal and our time together. Amen."

Through the meal, she caught his eye and shared a knowing smile.

After dinner, they moved to the living room for dessert. Nate cut generous slices of oven-warmed apple pie and topped it with vanilla ice cream, and they ate by the fire, the sweet cinnamon aroma filling the room. Contentment settled over her, the kind that came from being in the right place with the right people.

Nate was watching Emma with a fond expression. He caught Harper's gaze and smiled, and that same flutter that she'd felt when they first kissed now danced an allégro in her chest. This was what she wanted, what she'd been searching for—a place where she was loved and where she could love freely in return.

After dessert, Harper selected one of those cute little books—this one with sledding penguins—and helped Emma with her bedtime routine. They read the story together, and she tucked the little girl in. Then, leaving the room, she almost gasped over how easily she'd fallen into this role. It felt natural, like she was meant to be here.

Back in the living room, Nate took her hand and led

her to the couch. They sat close, the warmth of the fire and the crackling of the logs creating a peaceful atmosphere.

"Thank you for tonight." She leaned her head on his shoulder. "It's been wonderful."

He wrapped his arm around her, pressing his lips to the top of her head. "Hopefully, the first of many happy evenings together."

She liked the sound of that.

They sat in comfortable silence, the weight of their feelings hanging in the air. There were still challenges ahead, decisions to be made, but for now, she was content to be here, in this moment, with him. It was a beginning, and she would see where it led.

CHAPTER 18

As the weeks passed, Harper couldn't believe how different life was when she felt truly loved and accepted. She, Nate, and Emma spent all their spare time together, growing closer with each passing day. Harper had never felt so at home, so at peace.

One crisp morning, they bundled up in warm boots, coats, gloves, and hats and headed out into the fresh snow. With infectious excitement, Emma hopped around, eager to build a snowman. Nate and Harper laughed as they helped her roll large snowballs for the body and a smaller one for the head. Emma placed a carrot for the nose and used pebbles for the eyes and mouth. Harper had brought a scarf and hat to complete their snowy friend, and they stood back to admire their work.

"Looks like we have a new friend." Nate looped an arm around Harper.

Emma giggled. "Can we make another one?"

Harper smiled. "Of course, let's make a whole family!"

They spent the morning creating a snowman family, complete with a snow dog. Laughter warmed the air, and Harper couldn't remember the last time she'd had so much fun. By the time they were finished, they were all rosy-cheeked and tired, but their hearts were full.

On Sundays, they attended church together. Harper found solace in the services and the sense of community. Seeing Nate and Emma so connected to their faith helped her deepen her relationship with God. They often stayed after the service for coffee and conversation, and Harper enjoyed getting to know the other parishioners better.

She also spent time teaching Emma more ballet moves. They would clear space in the living room, and Emma's eyes would light up as Harper showed her new steps and techniques. Emma was a quick learner, and Harper found immense satisfaction in sharing her passion with her. Sometimes, Nate would join in, attempting the moves with exaggerated flair, making both Harper and Emma laugh.

One afternoon, Harper sat at the kitchen table, working on her quilting piece. With the fabric and threads spread out before her, she stitched the final details. The patch depicted her first trip to the island, the lighthouse, and the memories that brought her back each summer. It was a labor of love, and she felt deep accomplishment as she completed it.

Grace stopped by and checked on her progress. "That's beautiful, Harper. You've done an excellent job."

Harper beamed. "Thanks. I've had wonderful teachers."

Grace patted her shoulder. "We're all looking forward to seeing it in the community quilt."

As the Island Extravaganza approached, the organizing committee invited Harper to perform at the event. When she hesitated, Nate and Emma encouraged her to accept. The idea of dancing in front of the community left her trepidatious.

The day before the Extravaganza, Amber called, jolting Harper back into reality. A young dancer who'd recently joined the company had filled Harper's position. "I think Troy's up to his old tricks," Amber said.

Harper began thinking. Could she allow him to ruin another young dancer's life? She'd come to Sanctuary Island to rediscover herself, to heal, and to figure out what she wanted for her future. She hadn't come to hide and pretend the outside world didn't exist. Now that her life was on track and she knew who she was, a desire to expose Troy and save this young dancer from his coercive manipulation burned inside her. But any action would need to wait until after the Extravaganza.

Late the following afternoon, she stood with most of the townsfolk as the exhibits were about to be revealed. Nate hugged her to his side, Emma hoisted onto his shoulders so she could see above the crowd.

"When will they show the quilt, Daddy?" She craned around. "I want to see Grandma's quilt."

"It's not just Grandma's quilt. It belongs to everyone

on the island. It's a memorial to everyone who's ever been a part of our town."

"How can a quilt belong to many people?" Her little face pouted. "There's only one?"

Harper patted the girl's knee. "What your dad means is that everyone can think of it as theirs. It will be kept in the community center for everyone to look at so they can remember the people who helped make Sanctuary Island wonderful."

Mayor DeBruin's voice came over the sound system. They all turned their attention to the stage.

"Ladies and gentlemen, thank you for gathering together to celebrate our Annual Extravaganza. Each year is special, but this year's event is even more so. This year we commemorate the lives of the people who've contributed to this great place. The ladies of the quilting consortium have worked tirelessly to present their gift to the community, a gift that touches the lives and hearts of everyone here. I'd like to invite the brain behind this venture—someone who is always thinking of this community and its members—Mrs. Grace Hawthorn, up on stage to share her inspiration for the project. Grace?"

Grace walked casually onto the stage. For someone who was being highlighted, she handled it with ease, unaffected by the applause. She stepped in front of the curtain that blocked the quilt from view and took the microphone.

"Good evening, Sanctuary Island family. While I thank Mayor DeBruin for his kind words, I'm no different from anyone else here. I love this island and the people who live on it. This is our home, and this quilt tells our story. So, without any more ado"—she waved in the air—"the quilt."

The curtain pulled back, and there it was, beautifully framed in a border of blue, the colorful patches forming the island's shape, each one representing a family, a moment, a life.

Applause ripped through the hall as everyone gazed at their part of history etched in fabric and thread, time, and even blood from the pricked fingers. Harper looked at her hand and the memory of the momentary pain that was part of the process of making the quilt. No one would think of the effort that went into making it by just seeing it. Her life was like that, wasn't it? She'd suffered pain and dedicated her time and energy, but now, looking back, she couldn't see those moments, only the wonderful tapestry it created.

Nate squeezed her, whispering in her ear. "It's great."

"Thank you." She slipped her arm around his waist. "I'm going to remain a part of the consortium. My new hobby in my new hometown."

He grinned. "I like the sound of that."

"Thank you. Thank you," Mayor DeBruin said again as the applause died down. "Now we have another presentation. One as eagerly anticipated as the quilt, and from a member of one of the founding families. Another woman whose heart is fashioned from the soil of this island. Miriam Solheim. Miriam, the floor is yours."

Harper laughed as her aunt ascended the steps in her usual animated style. She was a character, always on stage, even when she wasn't, and Harper adored her for it.

"Thank you, Mayor DeBruin!" Aunt Miriam took the microphone. "I'll say what I have to after you all see what I've done. So, let's go."

The curtain swung back a second time, and Harper gasped at the beautiful sculpture. Crafted from clay and covered in epoxy, it depicted two dancers in motion. Harper could feel the fluidity in it. It was almost as if they were moving.

Tears were already in her eyes when she turned to the painting beside it. It was her.

A gasp escaped her lips. How was it possible? From the chaos of those early paint strokes, her aunt had captured her likeness perfectly. She met her aunt's gaze and blinked back moisture. Why would she do something like that?

Aunt Miriam smiled at her as she spoke into the microphone. "My inspiration for these pieces came from one of the biggest inspirations in my life. As you all know, I never had children, but for a long time, I watched my great-niece strive in her creative pursuits. She fought many oppositions to achieve her goals, and I prayed and rooted for her from a distance. Her struggles reminded me of those of the people who founded this island. The people who left what they knew to come to this paradise in the middle of Lake Huron.

"They didn't always have the approval of others. They didn't have the love and care of those they left behind. But they left anyway. They strove to make a better place for themselves and their families. Now, we get to enjoy the fruit of their labor. Like them, Harper has striven to find herself and her way in this world. This is my way of commemorating our founders, this island, and our new resident. Harper, I want to welcome you home, my sweet girl. Our new Sanctuary Island resident."

Fresh applause thundered, and Harper tried to hold back tears as words of welcome echoed from the other residents. In all her years of performing, she'd never had such recognition or such approval. Sanctuary Island was just that, her sanctuary. Her refuge. Choosing to stay was the best thing she'd ever done. She looked at Nate. His bright eyes shone at her. How could she have considered any other life?

"If I could have your attention, please," Aunt Miriam interrupted. "I have another surprise. Harper, as many of you know, is a professional ballerina. And to commemorate her choice to become one of us, she's been invited to perform this evening. And she has a very special partner. So, if you would allow them some time, please mingle a bit, and we'll soon enjoy the artistic movements of Miss Harper Mackenzie and Miss Emma Hawthorn."

Harper's heart pounded as Aunt Miriam made the announcement. It was time. She looked at Emma and her gleaming smile. "Come on."

Nate lowered her to the floor, and Harper took her hand.

"Go get 'em," he encouraged as he let her go.

Backstage, Harper helped Emma change into her leotard and tutu. She'd bought them matching outfits for the performance, and Emma could hardly stand still as Harper fixed her hair into a neat bun. She knelt before her. "Remember, dancing is about fun. I want you to go out there and show them how much fun you're having."

Emma flashed a toothy smile, nodding emphatically. Harper stood and led her to the wings to wait for the music.

Her heart thundered in her ears, sweat beading her brow. She took a deep breath. Emma stood on the other side of the stage, biting her lips. Harper waved at her encouragingly.

As the music started, her fear vanished. She leaned into the music, delving into the emotions and the story she wanted to tell. As she moved, Emma did her best to replicate her actions beside her, the little version of herself. Harper smiled at the enthusiasm and joy on her face and supported her when she faltered. Teaching Emma was a joy she couldn't describe, and dancing with her was more rewarding than any high-end performance with its full ensemble.

As the music faded, Harper's heart raced, the applause barely audible over the pounding in her chest. It was over. She'd performed, and her thudding heart felt light with relief.

~

NATE STOOD STILL, unable to speak as Emma and Harper performed. Harper was amazing, but Emma captured his attention. When she smiled, it was electric. Pure joy lit her face as if she'd found her one true pleasure in life.

Harper's influence was on display for the entire town. She truly was everything he needed, not only for himself but also for his daughter.

His heart stirred, a deeper love growing for the woman who was changing his daughter's life for the better. And his. She wasn't Bethany, and she wasn't better than his late wife, but she was perfect. Exactly who they needed. God hadn't broken his heart. He'd mended it in ways Nate never thought could happen. The pain of loss was gone, and only the joy of a new tomorrow remained.

EXHILARATION TUMBLED through Harper as she helped Emma change. The little girl couldn't stop talking about her performance, and Harper loved hearing it.

"Hey there, my beautiful dancers," Nate's voice interrupted Emma's chatter.

"Daddy, did you see me?" She cheered, rushing to him. "Did you?"

Nate lifted her into his arms and kissed her cheek. "You were amazing."

Harper stepped closer, and he looped an arm around her, kissing her in turn. "And so were you."

"Daddy, can I do it again?" Emma asked. Her hair was damp, but she looked ready to perform.

Harper knew that look—it was the one she used to have as a child.

"Do what, sweetheart?" Nate asked.

"Dance for people. It was so much fun. I want to do it again and again."

Nate looked at Harper, one shoulder lifting. "What do you think? Could Emma be your dance partner again?"

"Most definitely." Harper beamed. "I loved having her as my dance partner."

Emma reached for her, and Harper scooped her from him and into her arms, nestling her on her hip. Emma hugged her tightly, and she hugged her back.

There was a special place in her heart where Emma lived. Harper wasn't sure when it happened, but one day, she realized the love she had for Emma was almost as deep as the love she had for Nate. She kissed the little girl's cheek and turned to him as an idea came to her.

He took Emma from her, and Harper finished packing their things into their bag before going out to enjoy the rest of the festivities. Everyone praised the quilt and Miriam's art, but mostly they applauded her. Some parents even approached her about teaching their children.

It was the very thought that had come to her just before. Was this a coincidence? Or was God trying to tell her something?

CHAPTER 19

*G*race's birthday was always one of her favorite days of the year. This year, it fell on a Sunday, which made it all the more special. There was something about greeting the coming year in the house of the Lord. It was like having His blessing for what was to come. It may have all been her imagination, but even the singing seemed richer today.

She stood outside after the service, her mind and heart filled with the Lord and the hope of Christ. Her eyes turned to the door as Nate walked out with Harper, Emma swinging from their hands between them. She smiled at the new couple. More than a couple, they looked very much a family.

She sighed with content, thanking the Lord for answering her prayers. For years, she'd prayed for the fissure in Nate's heart to mend, and now she could see that it had. He was happier than he'd been in years, and

Harper was the cause. God sent the person who could mend his heart and whose heart he could mend in return.

Someone tapped her shoulder. "Good morning, Grace."

She spun. "Miriam, good morning. How are you on this lovely day?"

Her friend smiled. "Wonderful! I see you're watching our town's newest couple."

"I can't help it. They look great together."

Her son and Harper stood talking with Elijah and Sarah.

"That they do." Miriam watched them also. "I'm glad they found their way to each other."

Grace couldn't agree more. "It was a daily prayer of mine."

Miriam chuckled as she flicked her scarf over her shoulder. "Mine, too. Nate's the kind of man I always hoped Harper would find."

As Grace studied him, old memories surfaced. "He was young when he lost Bethany, and he struggled so much. She was an amazing woman who loved God, but for some reason, He called her home. He had a bigger plan for her. Nate didn't understand that for a long time, but I think he does now. I'm so glad he's found love again."

Miriam nodded. "God uses the hurts to make us stronger and show us His unfailing love by bringing greater into our lives than we could ever expect. I'm glad He doesn't work how we'd like Him to, but instead does what He knows is best for us. Even when we fight Him on it."

Grace laughed. "I second that. Nate was so resistant to loving again, but look at him. He's so happy."

Miriam nudged her. "Harper, too."

Grace would have liked to stay and chat. It seemed as if they hadn't talked in a long time, but she was expecting Nate, Harper, and Emma over for lunch. She had to get home if she wanted to be ready. "I have to go now, but why don't you come over for coffee tomorrow so we can chat some more?"

Miriam touched Grace's arm. "I'd love to. I'll bring muffins."

"I'll make the mochas."

Grace hurried home to finish preparing her birthday meal. It was a big deal in her house, and it would be Harper's first with their family. She wanted to make it special. She already had the raspberry-chocolate Swiss roll in the fridge for dessert.

By the time the family arrived, the table was laid. There was turkey-corn chowder, rotisserie-style chicken with roasted vegetables, mushroom risotto, her famous loaded mashed potatoes, and her imitation KFC coleslaw —Emma's favorite.

"Mom," Nate exclaimed at the spread. "You went all out."

She waved him off. "I wanted to ensure Harper had a special meal with us to celebrate my birthday."

"Thank you." Harper leaned forward and kissed her cheek. "But you didn't have to. It's your birthday, after all."

"I wanted to. And because it's my birthday, I get to do whatever I want." She ushered Harper to a seat beside her at the head of the table, while Emma sat on the other side.

"I see Harper's taken my place," Nate mused as he pulled out a chair beside her.

"I didn't think you'd mind the change." She seated herself and patted Harper's hand. "After all, she's the newest member of our family."

"Mom!"

Nate's bashfulness warned it was time to change the subject. "Why don't you say grace for us?"

They closed their eyes as Nate began to pray. "Heavenly Father, we give thanks for this new year of life for my mother and our family's new beginning. You've taken us from one season of life to another, and we thank You that You never left our side, even when we were tempted to leave Yours. Thank You, God, for everything. Thank You that Your love never fails. And thank You for this food, which smells amazing. Amen."

"Amen," they said together and began their meal.

They talked as they ate, and the day carried an added levity her birthday hadn't had in a long time. Grace was curious about how things were progressing with Harper. "Is everything ready for your move?"

Harper swallowed her drink and dabbed her mouth. "Not quite. I have a few things to deal with back in Toronto, but Nate's going with me to help."

Grace arched a brow at her son. "Is that so?"

"Yes. We haven't confirmed a date yet, but we're making plans. Harper's got a lot to settle there. Her apartment and her accounts. And the court case against Troy. But hopefully, it won't take more than a week or two to clear up."

"That's good." Grace squeezed Harper's hand. "I'm so glad you decided to press charges. Bullies like him should never be allowed to go free."

Harper shifted in her seat and nodded. "I'm not looking forward to it, though."

"I'm sure you'll do fine. Now, tell me, have you decided where you're going to live?"

"Miriam said I can stay with her until I'm ready. She likes having me with her."

"Of course, she does. Who wouldn't like having you living with them?" Grace eyed Nate from the corner of her eye. He met her gaze and flattened his lips to hide their twitching upward, but his eyes sparkled. Grace chuckled. If she were right, Miriam would soon be losing her housemate. Not that she'd mind.

Grace forked a bite of her chicken, savoring the flavor. "Harper, I've been asked several times about your dancing. People in town are keen to know if their children can learn."

Sighing contentedly, Harper sank back in her chair. "That's something I wanted to talk to you both about. An idea came to me after my performance with Emma. Several parents approached me afterward who wanted their children to learn, and I've been thinking about it since then. You told me once that I needed to have a purpose for my dancing if I wanted it to be fulfilling. I think I know how to do that now. There's a multidisciplinary program at the school where they teach various kinds of dance, but nothing specialized. I'd like to open a ballet school."

Nate beamed at Harper as Grace added her agreement. "That's a wonderful idea. We could use something like that here. We've never had a proper ballet school on the island."

Harper angled her head. "Never?"

Grace scooped another bite. "Not that can I remember."

Nate placed a hand on Harper's back, love filling his gaze. "It's going to be great."

Grace resisted the urge to gloat, but it was a hard task watching her son dote on Harper and keep a straight face at the same time. "Emma, why don't we bake some cookies while Daddy and Harper go for a walk?" She glanced at the lovebirds. "It's a nice day. You should enjoy it."

NATE'S HEART soared as he and Harper took the Ski-Doo to the lake. She rode behind him, her arms wrapped securely around his waist. He covered her hands with one of his, wanting nothing more than to be close to her.

They stopped at the lake, both getting off to sit at one of the picnic tables lining the shore. He slid the flask of hot chocolate from his bag and clattered it on the table. "Would you like a cup?"

She nodded. "Yes, please. I love your mother's hot chocolate."

"She loves making it for you. And she sent extra dessert for us, too." He set the container of cake beside the flask.

"Your mother thinks of everything."

He reached across the table for her hand. "Thankfully, not everything. But I'd like to think I get my inspiration from her when it comes to matters of the heart."

Harper's cheeks glowed. She was the most beautiful when she blushed.

He'd make her blush every day if he could. "I still can't believe you're staying. Are you sure? It's a big deal to leave your life in the city."

"Believe it. Sanctuary is going to be my new home." She quirked her brow as her free hand tucked her short hair behind her ears. "Why? Do you want me to change my mind?"

"Never."

The look in her eyes made his heart race. There was so much emotion there, like her heart was open before him. "I'm glad you asked me to go back with you to help clear things up."

"And I'm glad you're coming. I don't know if I could handle the court case if you weren't with me."

"I'm sure you would have, but I'm happy to support you and help stop that creep from abusing other women."

Harper had joined forces with Amber and several other dancers, and together, they'd pressed charges against Troy. They were due to give evidence at his preliminary trial the following week in Toronto.

Nate rounded the table to sit beside her, the sun shining down on them as he hugged her closely.

She leaned her head on his shoulder, and her body relaxed. He smiled, holding her hand and looking at their intertwined fingers. God brought them together and patched them like the quilt Harper helped create. Sometimes the past, the present, and the future wove together seamlessly, and only looking back, could you see how God stitched everything together. He was seeing it now.

"Harper," he whispered.

She hummed in response. "Yes?" She raised her head and peered at him. "Is something wrong?"

"No." He laughed as he pulled out a thin rectangular box from his pocket and removed his gloves.

Her eyes widened when he opened the box, revealing a delicate gold necklace, and then clipped it around her neck.

"What's this for?"

He eased back and tucked a wisp of hair behind her ears. "I wanted to give you something that conveyed my love."

She reached up and touched it. "You didn't need to do that."

"But I wanted to. We haven't been dating long, but I've fallen in love with you, and I wanted to give you something to remind you of that, every single day, whether I'm with you or not."

"That's so lovely of you."

When her eyes moistened, he leaned forward and brushed his lips against hers. "I want to make you happy. I want you to know you have someone by your side who'll be there through all the hurts, the joys, the ups, and the downs."

His voice clogged. He felt vulnerable and exposed, but if he hoped to build a life with her, he had to let the walls down. He had to open himself to the possibility of hurt, but also the possibility of tremendous joy, just as Elijah said. It was time he stopped living in fear and embraced the future God had for him.

Harper lifted her hands and gripped his shoulders. "I love you, Nate Hawthorn, with all my heart."

The urge to sweep her into his arms and hold her forever was overwhelming. He answered the only way he could. He pressed his lips against hers, drinking in the taste of hot chocolate as he snuggled her, and deepened the kiss.

EPILOGUE

a warm breeze blew through the open windows, the summer light shining down as Harper instructed her students. Dressed in her black-and-purple leotard, she paced the room, observing her little charges. The girls were at the barre ready to begin.

"Grand plié. First. Second. Third. Excellent! Again."

In the few months since the Sanctuary Pointe Ballet School opened, she'd been inundated with students. At first, she'd hoped to have one or two classes a week. Now, she had four sessions a week in the late afternoon, and another two early on Saturday mornings.

They finished their last positions. "Ladies, that's it for today. Give yourselves a round of applause. You did wonderful!"

The girls clapped, Emma standing amongst them. She ran to Harper once the class was over, hugging her.

Harper stooped to hug her back. "You did great, sweetheart. I'm so proud of you."

She dimpled. "Thanks. I practiced, just like you said."

Harper tucked Emma's curls behind her ears. "I can see that. You're doing so well."

"She is," Nate called. He stood by the door in his three-quarter khakis and a blue T-shirt with the activity center logo on the front.

"Nate! What're you doing here?" She hadn't expected him. She planned to take Emma for ice cream and then home.

He strode toward her and planted a kiss on her cheek before lifting Emma into his arms and kissing her, too. "I came to pick up my two favorite ladies."

"I thought you were swamped with visitors. It's the busy season."

He winked. "I'm never too busy for you two."

Emma giggled from her perch, and Harper joined in. "I'll get our things."

The smile refused to leave her face as she packed her travel bag. She loved her job, but she loved it when Nate came to pick them up even more. Especially today. She returned to them. "I've got everything."

"Great. We should get going. I have an important engagement later I can't miss."

Harper's heart sank. "I thought you were free, and that's why you came to pick us up?"

"I'm sorry, but as you said, it's the busy season."

Harper pressed her lips tight to hide her disappointment. Today was a special day, but Nate seemed oblivious to it. "I understand. When will you be finished? I can make something, and you can pick it up on the way."

"I'm not sure. It's an important meeting."

Somehow, she nodded her understanding as they set off.

The streets were overrun with people. Happy voices drowned out the birds and erased the memory of winter's quiet beauty. It was summer at its height, and everyone was hard at work serving the thousands of tourists inundating their shores. The hotel was open and fully booked, or so she heard, and Nate was busier than ever. She was adjusting to his long hours. They weren't getting to spend as much time together as before, but what time they had was special.

When she was a girl, she was oblivious to how hectic life was on the island at this time of year. She'd spent her days at camp unaware of the hard work the islanders put in to ensure everything ran smoothly. Now she was seeing the island as it was. Sanctuary Island residents worked as hard as or harder than those in the city. They carried the entire island on their backs and with the sweat of their brow. They were champions of their way of life, ensuring they preserved the health and happiness of all who lived and visited there. What a wonderful community she'd decided to make her home!

They dropped Emma off at Grace's house before Nate walked her to Miriam's. She was still living with her aunt, not that there weren't other options. They enjoyed each other's company, and Harper wasn't in a hurry to leave that sense of family to live alone.

He held her hand along the busy street. People were everywhere, wandering the island and taking in the sights. Trying to escape the hectic lives they left on the mainland to enjoy a slower pace, they overwhelmed the island. Harper chuckled at the irony. Their slow pace increased the island's pace.

"What's so funny?" Nate angled his head.

"I was just realizing how perspective comes into play in everything. The visitors come here for a slower pace, while our lives are turned upside down because of their presence."

He chuckled with her, stopping to take her chin between his fingers. "That doesn't matter. What matters is that, whatever pace there is, you're here with me." He gazed into her eyes before he kissed her.

She closed her eyes, savoring his gentle lips, wishing he didn't have to go back to work.

"Come on. It's getting late. I don't want to miss my appointment." He led her toward the house. As they strolled, they swung their hands between them like teenagers.

She smiled blissfully as she walked the street with the man she loved. She never had that with Troy.

Sentenced to three years' incarceration, her former lover was a distant memory, but in moments like this, she remembered him for teaching her a valuable lesson in love. Someone who truly loves you never tries to control or manipulate you.

Nate was the most considerate man she'd ever met. She squeezed his hand and rested her head against his shoulder. He wound his arm around her shoulders for the rest of their walk.

He dropped her off and hurried away, not even staying for the coffee she offered.

She trudged into the house and set her bag on the floor. Too grumpy to acknowledge Sir Greyson's cries for attention, she flopped down on the couch.

"Why the long face?" Aunt Miriam entered the room from the studio, wiping paint off her hands with a cloth.

"Nothing."

"And Sir Greyson is a Siberian tiger. What is it?" Aunt Miriam gave her a pointed look.

"It's Nate." Harper sulked. "He forgot my birthday."

"Did he?" Her aunt sat beside her. "Well, it's a busy time of year. Things can easily slip the mind. Once he gets a moment of quiet, he'll remember and call you."

"But—"

"Harper. Nate's not the kind of man to forget what's important to him. It must've been an innocent oversight. Give him a chance. Okay?"

Harper sighed. Her aunt was right. Nate wouldn't neglect those he loved. He'd taken the time to pick her and Emma up from the dance studio. That meant something. Surely, it was all just a momentary lapse. He'd remember.

"See. All better. You should go and have a shower and change before dinner." Aunt Miriam wagged a finger at her. "There might be something very special waiting for you once you're done."

Harper hopped up and kissed her aunt's cheek. "If anyone would remember, it's you. I'll go get changed."

She rushed from the room eager to try whatever sumptuous meal her aunt prepared for her. The wonderful artist was just as wonderful in the kitchen. Harper was learning a lot about cooking from her and Grace, each teaching her something of themselves in the process.

She stepped into her room but stopped, her jaw dropping. There on her bed was a beautiful midnight-blue Bardot dress embellished with diamantes on the sleeve. A matching pair of stilettos were on the floor. "Aunt Miriam!" She scooped up the note beside them.

Happy birthday, my love. I bought this outfit specially for you. I'll be back to pick you up in an hour. Nate.

Her aunt stood by the door, grinning, her arms folded over her chest. "See, I told you something special was waiting for you."

Harper twirled, unable to contain her happiness. "You knew about this?"

"Nate asked me to help him surprise you. And by the look on your face, I'd say he succeeded. I can't wait to hear what else he has in store for you tonight." She crossed the room and planted a tender kiss on Harper's forehead. "Happy birthday, my beautiful girl."

Harper sat elated as her aunt left. What surprises did Nate have in store for her? She was in a hurry to find out.

He arrived as promised and found her waiting—and so excited she could hardly keep still. It was her first birthday with him. No one had ever made her birthday special, not since she was a child.

"Hi, beautiful," he greeted, dressed in dark slacks with a light-blue button-down shirt and a midnight-blue jacket matching her dress. She drank in his appearance. He was more handsome than ever. And he'd even gotten a haircut.

The uncontrollable excitement threatened to make her giddy. "You look handsome."

He stepped toward her. "I had to match the most beautiful woman on the island if I wanted to be seen with her." He offered his arm. "My lady."

They left Miriam's house with her aunt's approving gaze following them. "It's a nice night," Harper commented on their stroll toward the shore.

"I hadn't noticed." His gaze fixed on her, he pulled her close and kissed her, sending a thrill throughout her body. Then he whispered, "I love you, Harper."

"And I love you," she replied, giddy, indeed. She didn't think of where they were going—she simply followed where he led. The location was nothing when Nate—the most important part of her day and the one who made her feel special—was with her.

Then the stately Shore View Palace stood regal before them, all white pillars and wraparound porches.

"Is this where we're going?"

He covered her hand with his. "I made a reservation."

They arrived at the restaurant and were shown to an outside table. The sky was streaked with the colors of sunset—amethyst, orange, and pink as the sun slowly dipped below the horizon. Just gorgeous.

Nate slid out her seat and then sat across from her. The main dining room was almost full, but he'd secured a secluded table for two on the patio overlooking the lake. With a gentle rustle, waves lapped against the shore.

He gazed at her adoringly. "Happy birthday, my love."

"This is the best birthday ever." Tears threatened her eyes.

Then the server approached, forcing her to take hold of her emotions. They ordered, and Nate insisted she have every course she wanted. He even said she could have two of anything she particularly liked. She refused, but the offer made her smile all the more.

"Close your eyes," he instructed after the server cleared their plates.

"Why?" What more did he have up his sleeve?

"Close. Your. Eyes."

She did as he asked, excitement again performing jittery practice steps inside her. What could it be? She heard the shuffle of feet and then the clunk of something being placed on the table.

"Now… open them!"

Candles. Dozens of sparking candles adorned a birthday cake with her name on it. There were so many she could hardly see Nate across the table.

She laughed. "You got me a cake?"

"Blow out the candles," he urged, and his excitement only increased hers.

She held her breath and then blew.

It took a moment for her to realize he was no longer in his seat, but kneeling beside the table in front of her, a small red box in his hands. In the center gleamed a stunning diamond ring. Her breath caught.

"Harper," he said in a soft voice. "I know this may seem soon, but to me, it's been a lifetime. I spent five years living half a life. Then you came into it, and suddenly, everything was better. You showed me what it was to love again, and through you, God taught me how to trust Him more. I don't need to wait any longer. I know you're the one for me. The only one."

He slid the ring from the box. "I promised you the day I gave you the necklace that I'd let you in. That I'd let down my guard and welcome you into my heart. And I have. Every part of it. There's no part of my life where you don't exist. You're my best friend. The person I want to see first thing every morning and last thing at night. And Emma adores you. We're a family, and I want that to be official."

He discarded the box and held the ring up before her. "It would be my honor if you would accept me as your life partner. To be my helper. My comfort. The best part of me. Harper Mackenzie, I love you with all my heart. Will you marry me?"

She could hardly see through her tears as Nate

confessed his feelings. Her hand trembled, but she held it out to him to place the ring on her finger. She couldn't speak to answer him, but her actions spoke for her. Of course, she would marry him. Being his wife was a dream come true.

He stood, pulling her with him and lifting her off the ground. He looked up at her and then brought her down, his kiss waiting to greet her. She fell into his arms and swore to never let him go.

Later, they walked along the shore. He carried her shoes, and the water lapped at their feet, cool and inviting. With her fiancé's arm secure around her waist, they approached the Solheim Lighthouse. Sailors used lighthouses to warn them of approaching land, but at that moment, the light seemed to guide their path into the future. The water washed away everything old as it tumbled into tomorrow, and they headed into their future together.

Harper gazed at her hand and the gleaming ring now adorning it as the moon hovered overhead. She closed her eyes as Nate grasped her shoulders, turned her, and gently kissed her lips.

"Happy birthday, my love."

But this birthday was more than a new year approaching—a whole new tomorrow awaited.

THREE MONTHS LATER...

Harper stood in Aunt Miriam's cozy living room, the

early fall air carrying a hint of the changing seasons. The morning had been a blur of final preparations and heartfelt moments with those closest to her.

Grace had outdone herself with the wedding gown. The dress, crafted with love and meticulous attention to detail, fit Harper's petite frame perfectly. The delicate lace overlay adorned with tiny pearls and sequins shimmered in the sunlight. The bodice hugged her figure, flaring at the waist into a flowing skirt that brushed the floor. She'd worn many beautiful garments in her role as a principal ballerina, but her wedding gown eclipsed them all. The intricate embroidery along the hem and neckline added an elegant touch, while the silken fabric felt luxurious against her skin.

Harper touched Grace's hand, stilling her last-minute adjustments. "There's no words, Grace, to thank you for all you've done. These last months, you've truly become like a mother to me."

Grace twisted her grip to hold Harper's fingers. "I'm sorry your mother isn't here."

Right. Harper's only regret was that her parents weren't there to witness her wedding. At the last moment, her mother had messaged that something urgent had come up and she couldn't make it. "But I'll be thinking of you," the message had said. Something more important, more like it. And her father? Harper hadn't heard back from him.

She squared her shoulders. "I can't say I'm not a little sad about that, but I'm okay." Her Sanctuary Island family provided her with all the love and support she needed. Her parents were missing out, Harper not so much. "Although I do hope and pray we might reconnect one day."

"It *is* a pity they can't see you. You look stunning, dear." Aunt Miriam fussed around her like a mother hen. "Nate's going to be speechless."

Sarah, Harper's matron of honor and new best friend, nudged her shoulder. "He won't know what hit him."

Emma twirled around in her white flower-girl dress, her basket of rose petals clutched in her small hands. "Do I look pretty, Harper?"

Harper bent and hugged her. "You look like a princess. The prettiest flower girl ever."

Sarah and Aunt Miriam completed the final touches, adjusting the veil, smoothing the lace, and ensuring everything was perfect. Finally, they stepped outside onto the porch. Harper's heart tumbled over itself as she approached the waiting horse-drawn carriage, her steps light with joyous expectation. Today she was marrying the man of her dreams. Her teenage crush. God had blessed her beyond her wildest dreams and given her love she never knew was possible.

The driver helped her into the carriage while Sarah held her veil before she, Grace, Aunt Miriam, and Emma joined her. Aunt Miriam's eyes glistened as the driver guided the horses along the street. Harper owed so much to her great-aunt, who'd welcomed her into her home with open arms and mentored and encouraged her over the months since Harper arrived on her doorstep, heartbroken and lost.

During the carriage ride to Sanctuary Bible Church, Harper felt like royalty. Familiar faces lined the streets—island residents who'd come out to witness this special day. They waved as the carriage passed, their warmth and support overwhelming.

Fall flowers and greenery adorned the chapel, and as Harper stood in the narthex alongside Aunt Miriam, the soft strains of a piano playing "Canon in D" reached her ears. She took a deep breath, the scent of the flowers mingling with the polished wood of the pews, as Emma began her walk down the aisle. The precious little girl whom Harper had come to love and cherish scattered petals with each step.

Next, Sarah moved forward, a picture of elegance and grace as she made her way down the aisle. Harper's heart swelled over the friendships she'd formed on this island. Genuine friendships to stand the test of time.

Aunt Miriam squeezed her hand before they moved forward. The rustle of her gown whispered with each step, matching the flutter of her nerves. As Harper neared the front, her eyes locked with Nate's. He looked dashing in his dark suit, his brown eyes alight with love. The world seemed to fall away, leaving only the two of them in a timeless embrace of love.

She handed her bouquet to Sarah, and then Nate took her hand and smiled into her eyes before they faced the front.

Nᴀᴛᴇ sᴛᴏᴏᴅ ᴀᴛ ᴛʜᴇ ᴀʟᴛᴀʀ, his heart pounding as he waited for Harper to walk down the aisle. People who'd shaped his life, the community who'd supported him through good times and bad, surrounded him. But today, he only had eyes for his bride.

Beside him, Elijah nodded his encouragement. If it hadn't been for his friend's wise counsel, this day might never have happened. Instead, Nate had taken the step of faith and declared his love for Harper. Letting go of Bethany hadn't been easy. The love they'd shared had been special, but now he shared a special love with Harper, one forged from brokenness and heartache, a second chance he'd never expected, much less dreamed of.

When Emma entered the sanctuary with her hair cascading in waves and her little face beaming, his throat clogged as love for his daughter rushed through him. Bethany would have been so proud. Emma scattered rose petals, and his heart swelled further.

Then Harper glided into the chapel and down the aisle, their gazes locked, and the world faded away. Her presence was a balm to his soul, soothing the lingering ache of loss to heal his heart. Taking her hands in his, he grasped the strength and warmth that had drawn him to her from the beginning.

Paul Solheim, a church elder and Miriam's cousin, began the ceremony, his profound words heartfelt, reflecting the deep faith that had guided Nate through his darkest times.

Soon, Harper gave her vows in a voice rich with love and conviction.

He looked into her eyes as he held her hand and said his vows from the depths of his heart. "Harper, you've brought light and joy into my life, healing parts of my heart I thought would never mend. I promise to love and support you and to be the best husband and friend I can be. You're my heart's desire, and with God's help, I'll cherish you all the days of my life."

After Paul pronounced them husband and wife, Nate took his time kissing his beautiful bride, not wanting this moment to end. They grinned at each other as applause resounded through the chapel.

At the lakeside reception, the late afternoon sun bathed the scene in a warm, golden light, reflecting off the water and creating a picture-perfect setting.

Later, under strings of colored fairy lights, he danced with his ballerina bride, and everything else receded into a blur of light and music, peace and contentment. Once the reception wound down, he led her by the lake. The breeze ruffling their hair, the waves lapped the shore, and the moon loomed on the horizon, casting silvery light over the water.

"I love you," he whispered, drawing her close and cupping her cheek.

She covered his hand with hers, the moonlight—or was that pure love?—shining in her eyes. "Not as much as

I love you. I thank God for bringing me back to this island, to this sanctuary, where I discovered not only who I am but also my one true love. You."

Heart soaring, he pressed his lips against hers, savoring the moment, but looking forward to all God had in store for them.

"FOR THE LORD IS GOOD; *his steadfast love endures forever, and his faithfulness to all generations" (Psalm 100:5).*

THE END

NOTE FROM THE AUTHOR

I hope you enjoyed "Tumbling into Tomorrow" and your journey to Sanctuary Island! Did you know that there are five more books in the **"Love on Sanctuary Shores" series?**

Tumbling into Tomorrow by Juliette Duncan
Fighting for Her Heart by Tara Grace Ericson
Surrendering to Love by Kristen M Fraser
Running into Forever by Jennifer Rodewald
Trusting His Promise by Valerie M Bodden
Wishing for Mistletoe by Robin Lee Hatcher

Find them all on Amazon!

And be sure to join the Small Town Christian Romance Reader Facebook Group to chat with the authors and other readers, and hear about new releases in this genre.

Lastly, I have a free gift for you! Join my Readers' newsletter (go to www.julietteduncan.com) and receive a free thank-you copy of "Hank and Sarah - A Love Story", a clean love story with God at the center.

Enjoyed "Tumbling into Tomorrow"? You can make a big difference. Help other people find this book, and this series, by writing a short review. Honest reviews of my books help bring them to the attention of other readers, and I'd be very grateful if you could spare just five minutes to write a few words!

Blessings and love,
Juliette

Find all of Juliette Duncan's books on her website:
www.julietteduncan.com/library

Beneath the Southern Cross: The Dawn of a Sunburned Land Series

Love's Unwavering Hope

A young woman forging a new life, an unscrupulous wealthy suitor, and a farmer fighting for her heart...

Love's Rebellious Spirit

She's abandoned her life of privilege. He's young and rash, but determined to provide for his headstrong bride, even if it leads them into the untamed heart of Australia...

Love's Distant Dream

From dust to destiny: an epic journey of love, loss, and legacy...

<u>A Sunburned Land Series</u>

A mature-age romance series

Slow Road to Love

A divorced reporter on a remote assignment. An alluring cattleman who captures her heart...

Slow Path to Peace

With their lives stripped bare, can Serena and David find peace?

Slow Ride Home

He's a cowboy who lives his life with abandon. She's spirited and fiercely independent...

Slow Dance at Dusk

A death, a wedding, and a change of plans…

Slow Trek to Triumph

A road trip, a new romance, and a new start…

Christmas at Goddard Downs

A Christmas celebration, an engagement in doubt…

True Love Series

Tender Love

Tested Love

Tormented Love

Triumphant Love

Precious Love Series

Forever Cherished

Forever Faithful

Forever His

Water's Edge Series

When I Met You

A barmaid searching for purpose, a youth pastor searching for love

Because of You

When dreams are shattered, can hope be re-found?

With You Beside Me

A doctor on a mission, a young woman wrestling with God, and an illness that touches the entire town.

All I Want is You

A young widow trusting God with her future.

A handsome property developer who could be the answer to her prayers…

It Was Always You

She was in love with her dead sister's boyfriend. He treats her like his kid sister.

My Heart Belongs to You

A jilted romance author and a free-spirited surfer, both searching for something more…

I'm Loving You

A young widow with an ADHD son. A new pastor with a troubled family background…

Finding You Under the Mistletoe

A beloved small-town doctor and a charming diner owner…

The Shadows Series

A jilted teacher, a charming Irishman, & the chance to escape their pasts & start again.

Lingering Shadows

Facing the Shadows

Beyond the Shadows

Secrets and Sacrifice

A Highland Christmas

A Time For Everything Series

A mature-age Christian Romance series

A Time to Treasure

She lost her husband and misses him dearly. He lost his wife but is ready to move on. Will a chance meeting in a foreign city change their lives forever?

A Time to Care

They've tied the knot, but will their love last the distance?

A Time to Abide

When grief hovers like a cloud, will the sun ever shine again for Wendy?

A Time to Rejoice

He's never forgiven himself for the accident that killed his mother. Can he find forgiveness and true love?

Transformed by Love Christian Romance Series

Because We Loved

Because We Forgave

Because We Dreamed

Because We Believed

Because We Cared

Billionaires with Heart Series

Her Kind-Hearted Billionaire

A reluctant billionaire, a grieving young woman, and the trip *that changes their lives forever...*

Her Generous Billionaire

A grieving billionaire, a devoted solo mother, and a woman determined to sabotage their relationship...

Her Disgraced Billionaire

A billionaire in jail, a nurse who cares, and the challenge that changes their lives forever...

Her Compassionate Billionaire

A widowed billionaire with three young children. A replacement nanny who helps change his life...

Heroes Of Eastbrooke Christian Romance Suspense Series

Safe in His Arms

Some say he's hiding. He says he's surviving.

Under His Watch

He'll stop at nothing to protect those he loves. Nothing.

Within His Sight

She'll stop at nothing to get a story. He'll scale the highest mountain to rescue her.

Freed by His Love

He's driven and determined. She's broken and scared.

Stand Alone Books

Leave Before He Kills You

When his face grew angry, I knew he could murder…

The Preacher's Son

Her grandmother told her to never kiss a preacher's son, but now she's married to one…

Promises of Love

A marriage proposal accepted in haste… a love she can't deny…

The Madeleine Richards Series (Pre-Teen/Middle-Grade Series)

Rebellion in Riversleigh

Trouble in Town

Problems in Paradise

ABOUT THE AUTHOR

Juliette Duncan is a *USA Today* bestselling author who is passionate about writing true to life Christian romances that will touch her readers' hearts and make a difference in their lives. Drawing on her own often challenging real-life experiences, Juliette writes deeply emotional stories that highlight God's amazing love and faithfulness, for which she's eternally grateful. Juliette lives in Brisbane, Australia. She and her husband have five adult children and eleven grandchildren whom they love dearly. When not writing, Juliette and her husband love exploring the great outdoors.

Connect with Juliette:

Email: author@julietteduncan.com

Website: www.julietteduncan.com

Bookstore: www.julietteduncanbookstore.com

Facebook: www.facebook.com/JulietteDuncanAuthor

BookBub: www.bookbub.com/authors/juliette-duncan

Made in the USA
Coppell, TX
18 December 2024

42910158R00163